MIDNIGHT SELF

MIDNIGHT SELF

ADRIAN VAN YOUNG

BLACK LAWRENCE PRESS

Black Lawrence Press

Executive Editor: Diane Goettel
Cover Art: "Creature in Yellow" by Michael Vincent Manalo
Book Cover and Interior Design: Zoe Norvell

ISBN: 978-1-62557-060-4

Published 2023 by Black Lawrence Press.
Printed in the United States.

The following stories in *Midnight Self* appeared previously in various forms in the following publications…

"Hammer" in *Granta* (2019)

"The Skin Thing" in *Electric Literature's Recommended Reading* (2014) and in *Gigantic Worlds: An Anthology of Flash Science Fiction* (Gigantic Books, 2015)

"Midnight Self" as "The Woman Who Bends" in *Black Warrior Review* (2014)

"Skin of Velvet, Buds Like Snow" as "Lady Winchester Deciphers Her Labyrinth" in *Masters Review* (2015)

"The Man Who Wore Death" in *Conjunctions* (2016)

"The Case of the Air Dancer" in *The Baffler* (2020)

"The Bachelor's Tale" as "The Bachelor's Tale, Which Goes Here Unrecorded" in *New Orleans Review* (2015)

"Long Pig" in *Mechanical Animals: Tales at the Crux of Creatures and Tech* (Hex Publishers, 2018)

"The Burial Party" in *Heavy Feather Review* (2019)

TABLE OF CONTENTS

HAMMER

In the commune, whenever I pick up a hammer to get through my chores on the board for the week, I feel like a killer, though not in a bad way, just capable, calm, like a killer should be.

But I'd never kill anyone in the commune. The people here are way too nice.

So I'm okay with seeing my name on the board with more chores beneath it than anyone else's. That is, after all, what I do in the commune: certain day-to-day maintenance, repairs and so forth that a hammer, though not always only a hammer, is usually needed to do to my liking. I don't resent the fact, for instance, that in dry-erase pen alongside Jax's name it only says, "DISHES—CLEAN, REPLACE." Or that next to Richie's name, right below Jax's, it says, "LAUNDRY—BEDCLOTHES," and next to that, "LIGHT BULBS." Or that in the space next to Anabelle's name, which Anabelle herself wrote out in big looping, vermillion cursive, it says, "DESSERT + SERENADE." After all, that's what Anabelle does in the commune; every night, she brings dessert. Then we eat it while Anabelle sings and plays to us on her old and rich-sounding acoustic guitar.

I don't resent Jax, who's the house president, who made the

chore-board in the first place.

Especially given that next to my name, spelled "ABE" instead of "Abraham" the way I like to hear it said, there are so many chores written after the colon, they drop down to the line below.

ABE: TOILETS—SCRUBMIRRORS— WINDEX DRAINS—UNCLOG FIREPLACE—SWEEP COMPOST— COLLECT AND DISTRIBUTE FOR MULCH FRIDGE—REPLACE FILTER(S)FRONT DOOR—INSULATE GUTTERS—CLEAR BOOKSHELVES— ANCHOR (PROTECT LITTLE RUBY!) LAZY SUSAN—REHINGEBACK GATE—LEVEL, RECALIBRATE LOCKFENCE—WEATHERPROOF SOLAR PANELS—HOSE OFF GARDEN—FENCE ROACHES—BAIT ATTIC STAIRS— REPLACE, REHANG....

My days are busy, busy, busy. I never put the hammer down. I carry it with me, attached to my belt. Its weight is constant, reassuring. And strange as it seems on the surface of things, that comfort is what makes me feel like a killer. Like everyone, probably, feels like a killer the moment they pick up a hammer, weight-test it: the satisfying calibration of the hammer in the hand; the stick of the grip; the cold heft of the metal.

Like they could kill at any moment, whether or not they felt the urge.

Today in the commune, I start with the quick stuff: cleaning the toilet, replacing fridge filters.

Zeke wanders in while I'm doing the toilets, takes a little half step and backs out toward the hall. I tell him I'll be just a second. So he shrugs and stands there with his arms crossed before him, leaning on the doorframe, facing into the bathroom, and when we've covered how he his, and how he slept the night before, and what he has in store today, which apart from the chores he has up on the board—"RABBITS—FEED" and "BIKE FLEET—PUMP"—apparently is not that much, I see him shift his posture sharply. I see he's got to go real bad. When I see that, I'm anxious for him and tell him just another second, yet not before asking him what's he been eating, not that it's any of my business. Because I just happened to notice, I say, that his bowel movements seem to come on him like thunder, which could mean he's getting a surplus of fiber or maybe too much fat, depending, and does he still smoke, in the morning, I mean, because that, too, could serve as a catalyst, maybe. Not that it's any of my business, not that I'm an expert. But.

All the while I'm scrubbing, scrubbing. Zeke stares at me patiently. He doesn't seem, quite, to know what he should say. I splash off the scrubber and let it drip dry; again, Zeke is venturing into the bathroom, faintly thrusting his hips with his hands in his pockets. I sense that he means to communicate with me. But it just looks like this little dance and sort of a rude one, if I'm being honest, like Zeke has a ferret loose inside his pants but like Zeke doesn't want me to know there's a ferret.

"All right." I nod slowly at Zeke.

"Yep," he says.

"Well," I say, "I'll leave you to it."

"That'd be great." Zeke laughs a little.

"At the non-profit—" I start to tell Zeke, but it's useless.

The bathroom door clicks softly shut.

I pause outside the bathroom door, the hammer hanging from my waist.

I shift my weight right, where the hammer hangs down. Then left, then right, then left again. I like this careful measuring between the hammer and non-hammer sides of my person because it confirms that the hammer's still there. When I left the non-profit, called Hands on Tomorrow, the place I worked before the commune, I took nothing with me except for this hammer. It has a word along the handle, the name of the tool's manufacturer: PLUMB. I've never heard of PLUMB before but whoever they are, they make excellent hammers. This one, I've found, has served me well, first at the non-profit and now in the commune. The name could hardly be more apt. On the one hand I find that it puts me in mind of precisely the image it means to evoke: a plumb angle between two beams, the gentle dropdown on a good flight of steps. On the other, however, it gives rise to something that was probably not intended by the company's owners: the fact that the hammer could be used for murder. So that when someone picks it up to put it to some broader use, it actually sways the mind over to murder— inexorably, like a clock tower's hand.

The hammer can't help that it does this to people. That's only how the hammer's made.

PLUMB, as in strike, on the top of the skull; PLUMB, as in distance, between thought and action; PLUMB, as in escape well made, are three unwanted connotations.

The commune that I live in is a renovated farmhouse surrounded by miles of open country. That's not to say it's isolated. Miles to the south is a sort of large town or a kind of small city, some people will tell you, which we commune-members can access by car or bike or sometimes hitchhiking; I guess it would make as much sense just to walk, though often as not people try to avoid it. You never know what you'll run into out there. Plus, the winters here are freezing. I arrived at the farmhouse in just such a manner, which is to say I came on foot, the miles of blank asphalt unfolding before me until, around this little bend, the farmhouse appeared, half-shrouded in fog. It was morning and early spring then in the country, with the birds waking up in the tops of the trees and a few early lights turning on in the house, which thinking back now could've been anyone getting ready to show their best face to the world: Jax, Richie or Anabelle; Coral, Zeke, Pierre, Big John; Sarah G or Sarah M. Strange to reflect on how well I now know them when back on that morning they weren't even people, just lighted squares showing themselves through the fog.

The first one I saw was Anabelle.

She was kneeling in one of the wood flowerbeds that line the front walk coming up from the road, wearing tan overalls with her hair in a scarf. Even hunched over like that in the dirt, she still had horn-rimmed glasses on and when she looked up at me, smiling of course, their lenses were fogged with garden moisture. She looked like she wanted to say something to me, she looked like she was going to greet me. Then Jax hurried out of the doorway above her and down the front steps with his head tilted up. "Hey, brother," he called to me. "How can we help you?"

In the kitchen downstairs I run into Pierre. Sarah G's with him. They're eating their breakfast: Pierre last night's leftovers mixed up with eggs; Sarah G steel-cut oatmeal with brown sugar on it and hunks of bananas. I greet them both, ask how they are, and how they'd slept the night before, and what they have in store that day, just as I'd asked Zeke in the bathroom upstairs, who I now hear above me, flushing.

Then Zeke washing his hands, tromping off down the hall.

Sarah G and Pierre give me cursory answers and go back to eating their breakfast in silence. I open the fridge and then close it again. They're hunched at the table, their backs to the fridge, so they have to turn toward me to hear what I'm saying, though only Sarah G does that; Pierre just sort of tilts his head.

I tell them I am pretty good.

I tell them I slept well enough.

Then I tell them, in terms of my plans for the day, that they are looking at them now and when they look at me unsure to what exactly I'm referring, not understanding, I suppose, that I have made a sort of joke, I clarify that what I mean is the ongoing replacement of the fridge's water filter and after that the composting and after that, maybe, securing the bookshelf, or maybe the bookshelf and then the composting, depending on what kind of mood I am in. Though probably, now that I really think of it, securing the bookshelf will have to come first. Jax underlined it, after all—and here I refer to the chore-board behind me—because it needs doing ahead of the rest and as house-president, we can only assume, Jax must hold the commune's best interests at heart. And besides (reason A), it will take a bit longer, involving the usage of anchoring pins, a drill, and several sets of brackets; and (reason B) it cannot wait, given the object, "PROTECT LITTLE RUBY!" Anabelle's two-year-old daughter, the only child the commune has, who likes to climb on everything and sooner than later will get to that shelf.

That's all by way of saying, I add, already it's a busy day.

"There you go," says Pierre and turns back to his breakfast.

Sarah G smiles politely. "Sounds like it," she says.

"Busy, busy," I say in a little singsong. "Busy, busy," I say, and

6

reopen the fridge.

Inside is a chaos of Tupperware cartons and carryout boxes and old plastic bags that likely contain vegetables from the garden, and amid everything are these tiny half-nubbins without any protective wrapping: half an apple, insides browning; a congealed bowl of jelly or gravy or something that jiggles a bit when I poke at the rim. Anabelle's yogurt parfait of that morning with its sparkling raspberries and mangoes on top.

As I pop out the housing that safeguards the filter, unwrap the new filter and extract the old one, I'm talking back over my shoulder at them about different ways of arranging the fridge. I've learned a thing or two, I say, not just from my years as a practiced fridge-owner but at the non-profit where I worked before in a similar role as my role in the commune. That included odd jobs, like the scrubbing of toilets and the hinging of doorframes just like I do here, yet also more day-to-day matters of service, you might even say the public good, like noticing something amiss in the fridge and taking mere seconds to straighten it out. At Hands on Tomorrow, the place where I worked, when I went to the fridge and I found it like this, I didn't do what one might think, throwing out food that I judged past its prime or food that sat unclaimed by someone but rather would arrange the food on the three tiers of fridge in the following order: the top tier—food that could go bad and so must be eaten within a day's time; the middle tier—food that was still in its packing and had a grace window of two days or more; the bottom tier—personal bundles of food that would more or less certainly vanish post-lunch. This way, I say, without much effort, the fridge became something much more than a fridge. It became, well, a sort of conveyor belt, really, moving food in and out, moving food in and out, moving food in—

I stop for three reasons at this point.

One: I have conveyed my point.

Two: I must concentrate, however briefly, on the miniscule work of exchanging the filter.

Three: Pierre has gotten up in the middle of our conversation, clattered his breakfast things into the sink, presumably for Jax to wash, and left the room for somewhere else.

Sarah G, I sense, remains, though the sound of her eating her oatmeal has ceased. The last couple clicks of exchanging the filter are deafening there in the mid-morning kitchen. Finally, I turn around.

The hammer turns with me, attached to my belt. The claw tangles up in my baggy pants fabric, creating a crotch-aligned pulling sensation which isn't unpleasant, if I'm being honest, while the handle of the hammer, anchored rigid by the claw, presses insistently into my leg. It's an awkward phenomenon wholly at odds with the sinuous grace of the object itself, which could fit in the hand. Which could tip through the air.

She's facing me now, her bowl empty before her. Her eyes are wide and glazed with something—not interest, not boredom, but something alarmed I vaguely recognize as terror. The fridge shuts of its own accord, the sound of the gasket seal making us jump, and it's like at the non-profit Hands on Tomorrow, in the break-room/ lounge with the cracked water-cooler, and the dull yellow couch, and the fridge in the corner where all the workers stored their lunches, and I would come into the break-room/lounge, striking up small talk like everyone did, like everyone does in a break-room/ lounge, as though that's somehow not the purpose—and not just tips or need-to-knows, but harmless, nice stuff like the news or the weather, and as I spoke I had the sense of bodies dispersing in space/time behind me, downing and throwing out used water cups, miming the ends of conversations, zipping up lunch-pails and slinging them on, and when I turned around again it would only be me and one fellow still there, an office assistant who only spoke Spanish, and his face would look at me like Sarah G's face, like Sara G's face appears now in the kitchen, a little confused and a little afraid but overall receptive to the prospect of connecting and I would start in on, you know, just something, while the fellow sat there at the table and listened.

"At the non-profit—" I tell Sarah G, but before I can tell her the truth, she says, "Sorry." She gets up, deposits her bowl in the sink. At the door, she turns back and explains to me, "Work. The mid-shift."

Then she's gone.

I put my money where my mouth is, start doing my best to reorder the fridge.

When I'm done, I close the door and stand staring into the shiny fridge metal—the magnets for takeout, ERACISM, Greenpeace, Gryffindor from *Harry Potter,* which I happen to know is Anabelle's and I center it slightly, a smile on my lips. Because it can't hurt, I reopen the door and clear out some space on the top, urgent shelf. There between some chicory and Richie's leftover goat-cheese enchiladas, I cradle the hammer down onto the shelf, close the fridge again, stand back.

I track five minutes on my watch.

I open the door to the fridge a third time and lift the hammer from the chill. I cradle it, feeling the different parts of it—the grip, faintly viscous at forty degrees the claw and the head, which are cold to the touch. The head especially intrigues me, the cold embedded in it now almost enough to sting the skin, the makeup of its molecules reordered in minutes, a different thing from what it was. It's almost like, how do I say this exactly, replacing the hammer again on my belt, the hammer was one way, but now it's another. Just like how a person can be one kind of person before feeling the weight of the hammer in hand yet then, when they've felt it, become someone else.

The room-temperature object turns into a cold one. The person ceases to exist.

The bookshelf's in the common room. Anabelle's reading in there on the couch. She's often there reading to herself or to Ruby on mornings or afternoons when she's not working. She's part-time at this chocolatier/espresso bar-place she brings us treats from when she works on "dessert nights," like she's some kind of hippie mom, limiting our sugar intake, although Anabelle never enjoys them herself. She only eats "clean foods," like nuts and raw carrots and once in a while those parfaits that she makes. Today, she crunches celery behind the bent spine of the book that she's reading, some sort of gargantuan fantasy novel with dragons and wizards and trolls on the front. She lies along the sectional in a cardigan sweater and paint-splattered jeans. She looks up when I enter, says, "Hey, Abraham." Smiles warmly and goes back to reading her book. She's got this pink streak in her hair.

I like that she calls me Abraham. I like the climate of her smiles.

I like the songs she writes and sings in the post-dinner hour on her old Gibson standard, songs about dragons and wizards and trolls that seem to emerge fully formed from the books about dragons and wizards and trolls that she reads. I'm always just outside the door to the bright common room where the commune sits listening, taking breaks between bites of their malt balls and truffles to murmur their thanks for this creature among them, and I murmur mine, too, although nobody hears me.

Völlkingkraft the Wizard came

to lay the dragon looooow
And Völlkingkraft went on his way
beneath the full moon's gloooow

Though it would be fair to call Anabelle "pretty," maybe even "desirable" under her clothes, most of the time I can't think of her that way. It almost feels wrong for some reason, I mean. Or maybe like I'm being stupid, failing to see the part of her that matters, this "lovingkindness" (Jax's term) that Anabelle carries wherever she goes. It seems to beam out of her Gibson's sound-hole like one of those fiery red Jesus heart portraits, blinding the looker with heavenly grace. In these moments, listening to her, she makes me feel not like I might float away. But like I'm immovable, permanent—stone.

I want to tell Anabelle so many things. I want to tell Anabelle: At the non-profit.

I want to tell Anabelle: At the non-profit, and have her stay to hear the rest.

I want to tell Anabelle: At the non-profit, called Hands on Tomorrow, where I worked before, an organization begun by do-gooders to get ex-cons back on their feet, of which I was one and still technically am, when I would walk into the break-room and everyone else in the room would start leaving, it was only Eduardo, the man who spoke Spanish, who stayed to listen to me talk. Eduardo was dark and short and beefy, with his short hair gelled forward and into this peak. Beneath the nice clothes that he wore in the office I could always see traces of many tattoos, though on the few times that I saw him outside, on the way to the carpool that brought him to work or picking up his daughter at school or coming home again at night from this little dive bar where he went with his friends, I never didn't see him in a heavy metal t-shirt because that, I suppose, was the music he liked. And I want to tell Anabelle: at the non-profit, between the hours of twelve and one, Eduardo would sit there, attentive and decent, smiling at me though he half-understood, and I would give him every gift that experience placed in my power to offer. And I want to tell Anabelle: At the non-profit, when me and Eduardo would talk during lunch, how I would take my tool belt off and drape it across the back part of my seat, just like I do sometimes when Anabelle's singing, and how sitting there in the break-room together would flood my being with relief. It was me who was sitting there, me who was present, and nothing could change that, not even the hammer.

I want to tell her all of this but I just walk past her and circle the shelf.

It's a secondhand bookshelf hauled in off the street by presumably Jax, who's the house treasurer and likes to procure all our furniture that way, from a slough of old wreckage infested with bedbugs. And I'm not exaggerating when I say the word bedbugs. On my last list of chores on the dry-erase board, "IMMOLATE OLD MATTRESSES" had been first.

I'm inspecting the bookshelf when Jax stumbles in followed by Little Ruby, who's tugging his shirt. Anabelle looks up and smiles when they enter. She tents her book and spreads her arms and Ruby runs into them, howling and laughing.

"Mother of dragons!" says Jax and sits down on the end of the sectional couch near her feet, and Little Ruby knows the word. She flaps her arms. She breathes fake fire.

"What tidings?" says Anabelle.

"Torching some kingdoms." Anabelle frowns. "And, you know, helping people."

They're sweaty and dirty from playing outside where Jax will take Ruby on Anabelle's off-days "to give her a second to breathe," he announces, even though I have secretly come to believe it's less for her sake than it is to impress her. But Anabelle lets them; I guess I can't blame her. Anabelle's a single mom. Everything depends on her—Ruby's meals, Ruby's school, Ruby's sheets being clean—and never more on days like this when they've got nowhere else to be.

Only then does Jax look up and notice I'm there.

Though I'm still facing toward the shelf that leans on the adjacent wall, I can feel Jax's eyes on me blue and assessing, before he announces, "Hey, Abe! Toddler-proofing?" I nod at the shelf, but I still don't respond. "Abe's a beast with the chore board," says Jax to my back. "Hell, Abe is johnny-on-the-spot."

"Johnny spot!" cries Little Ruby.

Jax wears a pair of drop-crotch harem pants. Jax hardly ever shaves his face. Jax's t-shirt is holey and stretched at the collar. Is Jax wearing shoes? Jax is close to the earth. Jax's hair is shoulder-length and progressively griming itself into dreads. Jax is talking to me—not about me, but to me. Still, I don't dare turn around.

Or it's not even that; I've got other things going.

I'm poking around the backside of the bookshelf, studying how it leans up on the wall so I can gauge where best to mark for the holes that will square with the ends of the anchoring brackets.

"Anyway, Abe," Jax says to me, "glad you're finally getting to this. I underlined it on the board? To like, you know, prioritize it? For the tiny among us," I hear Jax stage-whisper with something playful in his voice, and I turn to the side just enough to make out that he's grinning at Ruby, hand cupped to his mouth. "So, like, *did* you see it?"

I tell him I did.

"Did you see it was underlined, though?"

I nod at him.

Jax says, "Okay, well if you did—"

Anabelle clears her throat before Jax can go on. "I'm pretty sure he saw it, Jax."

I want to turn around so bad. I want to see her face so bad.

To see her roll her eyes at Jax who doubts my commitment to Ruby's safekeeping or see her kind of shrug at me, like whatever it is that bothers Jax I shouldn't give a second thought. I want to hear her say my name, like she said it before, the nice way that I like or like I've heard her, late at night, say Jax's name in Jax's room behind the wood of Jax's door when Little Ruby's fast asleep, a whisper, fierce yet also whiny, like Jax is performing some small, needful surgery on Anabelle while she's awake, and I stand there outside the door with my hammer and tool-belt, listening closely, until I can't stand hearing them anymore and I move in my sockfeet along the dim hall.

Holding the bracket against the drywall, I take a pencil from my tool-belt and mark through the holes at the end of the bracket where the anchoring pins will go into the wall. I move to the opposite side of the shelf to repeat the procedure when Jax is behind me—so light, just his palm, at the base of my shoulder.

"Abe, my dude, is that the stud?"

I tilt my head slightly so Jax sees my profile.

"I mean," says Jax, "like, I'm no expert, but don't you have to find the stud? Otherwise, it won't work, right?"

I turn to face Jax then, I summon a breath. I proceed to explain myself slowly and calmly. How while Jax isn't incorrect, that the stud inside your average wall is good to find in certain cases, like maybe, say, for hanging pictures between fifteen and twenty lbs or installing the hardware to hang curtains rods if the molding for some reason isn't an option, in the case of this bookshelf with dozens of books just waiting to crash on and hurt Little Ruby, to anchor it into the drywall directly with the anchoring pins and the two metal brackets will best the stud for several reasons—a term, "best the stud," that I actually use, my eyes turning meaningfully up into Jax's. First the brackets and the pins, which open like hollow points into the wall are more loadbearing, actually, than the decades-old woodwork in most older houses; and second for aesthetic reasons, like keeping the shelf where it currently sits between the far end of the sectional couch and the ottoman chair beneath the window, it would be better overall to let us determine the shape of the room as opposed to the stud, an inanimate object or not even an object, really—a piece of hidden infrastructure, keeping the wall-frame from tumbling down.

But Jax only looks at me blankly, says: "Right."

A hammer is more than a handyman's tool. A hammer also has a face.

Not a figurative face, but an actual one, as anyone well versed in hammers can tell you or as any good hammer-anatomy chart can show you clearly, part by part. The top of the hammer, that's the head. The seam at the top of the head is the eye. The flat parts that border the head are the cheeks. The front of the hammer continues this theme: the upper curve is called the throat, the lower curve is called the neck. The perfect flat circle that widens again from the curve of the neck and the throat is the face. Or anyway that is thetechnical term. Although I like to think that the hammer entire, from handle to head, is a visage of sorts—a portrait of a living face that is sometimes my own and sometimes someone else's.

On the Common Room couch, Little Ruby looks bored. She's clicking her jaw while picking some dirt from her toe cuticle. Her mother, however, is staring right at me, not with alarm but a plaintiveness, maybe, this shining heart-pain in her eyes.

I see the look come up in her but don't have time to ask her what.

I don't have time to say to her, "At the non-profit..." because Anabelle's already gathering her things: her glasses, her sandals, and finally her daughter. She says to us only, "I'll leave you guys to it," before she leaves the room completely, and it's like the non-profit all over again, the last day I ever walked into the break-room and everyone started to pack up their stuff, but how this time Eduardo, my sole confidante, my patient absorber and, maybe, my friend, began to pack his things up too with a secretive urgency, rustling and zipping, like he didn't want me to know he was leaving as I stood at the fridge rearranging its contents, talking back over my shoulder to him about how my system of storage had worked, the fridge was that much roomier, that much less crammed with rotten things, yet how, as I spoke, I was tracking his movement from the door to the break-room and out toward the hall. I left the fridge to block the door. I think I even held his hand. I could smell his hair gel and could see his pores shining. He'd had something with onions and garlic for lunch. And it's like I'm still there with him, blocking his way, the hammer hanging from my hand.

Jax is knocking on the drywall, trying to find the dense sound of the stud. I make the marks to set the pins. One side of the bracket will sit on the pins, with the screw going in through the hole in the bracket and into the teeth of the anchoring pin, where it will lodge inside the drywall, impossible to shake or jar. As I'm making the second mark Jax holds my hand. "Don't you need a drill for that?"

"No," I tell him. "Too much plaster." Shaking Jax's hand from mine, I gesture at the dark grey carpet. I cringe at the thought of it flecked with white specks, like a splatter of blood on a newly white wall.

Several taps with the hammer, I say, are sufficient to ease the pins along their way and then I ask him will he hold them, right here, on the mark, while I finish the job.

THE SKIN THING

When the Skin Thing, we called it, first came to our doorstep, the growing season was upon us. The only thing we grew were onions. We had come to Oblivia, hoping for better, but onions were all that would take in the soil. A pox of dry-rot on our ships, parts of them flaking away in the sandstorms. We could not breach the atmosphere to return to the carbonized husk of our planet, though the option was one we still wanted to have.

The colony soured, with expired-milk complexions. The allotments we tended were sallow and scuffed.

The Skin Thing dragged itself along on two great stalks that looked like elbows. Imagine a person, out prone on the ground, that drags himself by fits and starts. The elbows strove to gouge the earth, as sharp and tall as circus poles, and they levered the body along by great drags. Its head stuck out eyeless, oblong as a horse's. Behind the elbow-things it used to drag itself across the ground there stretched like a laundry sheet strung out for drying a tensile wall of thick pink skin.

It was the height of foursome men, and its body behind was a languishing tube, and its head, although eyeless, was snouted, with nostrils, that sucked and blew as it grew near.

Just one of us, McSorls, held ground. He was seeking, we think, to protect his allotments. It plucked him up inside its mouth, like the mouth of a puppet, and gobbled him down. Or gummed him down. It had no teeth. The leg of his pants dangled out, disappearing.

The Skin Thing ate his onions, too.

And every several months or so, when the onions turned over their blooms into bushels, the Skin Thing would come on its elbows, with huffs, to take a couple more of us.

It was, to us, a kind of God.

Especially now, with a famine upon us, where every onion was a feast and every extra mouth to feed another Skin Thing come to bleed us.

The mission had gone wholly wrong. Oblivia, and here to stay. We grew what we could and we ate it. Committees. We groaned ourselves to sleep at night. For scenery we left the camp and walked among the scorching sands.

The sun went down each day three hours but other than that the heat boiled off our blood. The night was a false one: a burnt orange dusk. And fourteen moons in place of stars.

How we colony members would placate the Skin Thing, so early on, was clear to us. It was not done by lottery. It was not done by penal system. It was done by the most sober practice to hand: which colonists produced the least.

We didn't restrain them, these Under-Producers, but commanded them rather to stand in one spot with the tacit restraint of our eyes centered on them and as the sun that was not ours began to go down in a sky that was neither, the Skin Thing would lurch from the regions beyond and would stop, taking scent, at the farthest allotment.

It ate a couple nearby onions. Or maybe it took up no onions at all. Just as sometimes it ate the appointed right there or would save him for after it left as a snack. And then, mournfully, it would rotate around with a vast and unknowable sadness upon it and would lumber away through the barren white sands by what trackless instruction we little but knew.

The Under-Producers it didn't eat there had a habit of looking behind them unsure, as though to ask us: must we still? But we too had a habit, which was to hold hands, and to all close our eyes, and to sway, humming faintly. And when this person saw at last he was no longer welcome among his own kind, he would follow the Skin Thing and we would just watch them—the Skin Thing ahead and the doomed one behind until they had crested the planet's horizon.

Until they were no longer ours.

McSorls came first. McGaff. McShea. McVanderslice. McGuin. McGreaves…

Colonists total: two-hundred and forty.

Colonists fed to the thing: thirty-six.

Colonists saved on account of this practice (not to mention the onions): one hundred, at least.

Life was, for an instant, as right as it could be.

Until the matter of McGrondic.

He being, McGondric, just one of our number, just any of us in the years since McSorls—but a father, he was, in the full flush of life, which was curious to us, so leached of our own.

There was—

McGondric in the mess, picking over his onions in no special hurry, a relaxed, dewy look to his under-eye skin.

McGondric going through the camp with his harvest of onions arrayed under cheesecloth, and heavens, his basket, the way that he bore it: offertory, slimly poised.

McGondric alongside his daughter, McGale, as they raked up the sands that comprised their allotment, their pink, sleek arms pushing, and pulling, and pushing.

Pursuant these sightings, we studied McGondric—his comings and goings, the hours that he kept. Not only in public, as on past occasions, but when McGondric didn't know—when McGale *and* McGondric, the daughter, the father, were all alone inside their home. This house, in the way of Oblivia's houses, was up upon stilts for the copious storms—shrieking behemoths of wind and white sand that tore across the fallow steppe—and McGale and McGondric would putter about it, there against the backlit pane.

But time after time, they were not in the house. We could not see them through the window. They were not lying down; we accounted for that.

And we wondered: McGondric, McGondric. Where is he?

Where is McGondric, when we are just here?

When at last on a day when McGale and McGondric were weighing their yield in the Harvesting House, we curious few of Oblivia crept to the edge of the house where the two of them lived. One person among us—Mc-something-or-other—began to claw amid the sands. He uncovered a window to somewhere illegal—a cellar in McGondric's plot.

And there, behind the sandy glass, we saw a crown of human head.

And under it: a hand. A knee.

We rubbed away more to reveal the whole person—McShea, we recall, was the first one we saw—and next to McShea there were fifteen odd others in an underground room about fifty feet square. There were struts at the corners to bear up the ceiling and the floor was made out to the foot with grouped palettes. Across these palettes, in the dim, an encampment of bodies did not stir.

We figured: they are eating them. And that is why they look so well. McGale and McGondric are hale and well kept, like the Skin Thing is kept, on the roughage of lives.

But when we broke into McGale and McGondric's, going down a trap door that led into the cellar whose insides the buried glass pane had revealed, we came up with McGaff, McShea, McVanderslice, McGuin, McGreaves.

All but a few of the Under-Producers we had banished to die were still here, still alive. That was why there was a window, so the Under-Producers could still see the sun.

These same Under-Producers, now captives, we held. And a great many of them, we threw in the sand. And a good portion too of these many we kicked and punched about the head and neck.

McGondric, the fairest among us, the freshest. McGondric of nights spent at home, mending drapes. McGondric, who had journeyed out when the sun of Oblivia sank for three hours and in that otherworldly dusk had discovered the Under-Producers still walking, one by one stepping over the frail, bleached remains of those who had followed the Skin Thing before them and died of exposure out there in the wastes. McGondric, the softest among us, the kindest, where all of us had grown so hard—who had gone to each one of the Under-Producers that the Skin Thing had not gobbled down on the spot, banished to walk undigested and lost beyond the borders of our mercy, and had hid them, and fed them, and kept them from us. McGondric himself, who had lately returned to the house upon stilts where he lived with his daughter to find us waiting for him there, prostrating the people McGondric had saved. McGrondric, whose gorgeous complexion came not from the rabid consumption of colonist flesh but from the milk of love and grace, so long expired in all of us.

All this we knew but did not say. All this we glimpsed but did not see. No more than we asked why the Skin Thing unsated—or sated far less than we'd come to believe—had never returned to destroy us completely but seemed to respect our dominion as ours, gumming one of us down only when it felt like it while others of us it cast loose to the wastes. Why the Skin Thing was habit-less, trackless. Unlike us. Ravenous one day, indifferent the next.

And so McGondric, too, we held. McGondric, too, we kicked and punched.

What had made him commit such untenable treason?

What had made him not do what had always been done?

McGondric didn't say: please don't. McGondric didn't say: you fools.

He only said, "Because I must." And turned to look upon McGale.

Well, McGale dropped her doll, and she ran to her father, we were sure to embrace him amidst his disgrace, but we all made a sound when she reeled back and hit him—and hit him again and again on the breast. She was cursing her father, "You promised! You promised!" beating with her small, fierce fists.

Yet that didn't stop us some days after that, when the Skin Thing arrived at our doorstep again, from marshaling hence all these Under-Producers and leading them out once again to their fates.

And that didn't stop us from seizing McGondric, and seizing his daughter, McGale, in due course, and having them follow the Under-Producers like fisher-folk crossing a river of ice.

And that didn't stop us from closing our eyes to the way that the daughter walked clutching her doll, and with her other hand

McGondric's, and how the doll itself hung there, a derelict and listless thing.

Though really, we told ourselves, grouped in a phalanx along the far edge of the furthest allotment awaiting the God at whose altar we worshipped in raptures of boredom and dissatisfaction, we had closed our eyes not on the daughter McGale, but the Skin Thing at large as it dragged itself toward us.

It writhed its head that did not see. It gaped its mouth that had no teeth. And it shuddered the skin-wall connecting its hackles that was in truth not skin at all, but a cell density that was alien to us.

Yet we couldn't see any of this, as we said.

Our eyes were closed. Our hands were linked.

And that was what stopped us from seeing at last that the Skin Thing was already moving away, that the Skin Thing, abhorrent, was too far to reach us—just a man and his daughter and many beside who had known themselves lost and too long to our mercy, and who knew before even we knew, and we did, that life as we lived it could only get worse.

MIDNIGHT SELF

Moira wakes at three a.m. from a series of plodding and linear dreams to the voice of a woman not herself speaking over the snow of her son Theo's monitor.

It says: "… eyoo… eyoo … esp … o … aaayit … isss … thee … o … rrr … sssrrt…"

The receiver lights up like a whippoorwill's eyes, casting red haze on her husband Paul's cheek. She reaches for him, draws up short.

The voice, it is surely a woman's, speaks on. "… greeor … bu … duuu … miankre … wusuhaiii … mmm … gette … riiimes …"

The monitor is analog. It is smelted together from shells of hard plastic. It has dials, LED, and a frequency band designed to squeeze out interference. Paul, too, is waking; he's powering on. *Again*, Moira thinks. *It is happening again.*

"Your round?" Paul sort of shouts at her.

"No rounds!" She is already half out the door. "There's some-one—a stranger—in Theo's room, Paul. There are no fucking rounds," she says.

"Why didn't you say that—"

But Moira is gone. The dim parallax of the hall is before her.

It narrows then roams with peripheral fuzz, judders as she starts in running. She has not arrived in her son Theo's room, but nor has she taken the monitor with her and she moves in a cognitive dead space, a void, where an impotent panic begins to set in. She passes the pictures, like dim portals, shining. Goes under the rope-pull that opens the attic. Turns left at the dark at the top of the stairs across whose width a baby gate is dividing the landing below into channels.

At Theo's door she turns around to see her husband lurching toward her, one of his hands pushing into his eyes, the other one feeling the plaster for balance.

She takes in a breath like a breath during labor—*an organizing breath,* she thinks—and she levers the door handle down, the door in. It reveals her baby's bedroom like a slow wipe in a film: the toys, the box-assembled crib, the nautical theme of the mobile, revolving. At first there is darkness above Theo's crib, a bank of darkness, hovering there, in which nothing of him or his life can be seen.

But then she hits the bedroom lights and the depth of it comes into view, with him in it.

Instantly her son starts crying, face disintegrating in something like umbrage. And instantly, instinctively, she scans for the rash that only several months before had threatened with fever his tender brief life. First his elbows, then his knees, before moving on to his knuckles and eyes, and diminishing finally in muscle fatigue that left him weaker, more exposed. A runt of immunity, bare, on a mountain. The illness is called JDM—Juvenile Derma-something-something; a name that Moira can't pronounce. Since Theo arrived home from Children's last week, tonight is their first with the monitor on. Moira has crashed in his room like a drunk the last seven nights.

Moira goes forward. "Hey Theo. Hey, you. It's Theo's witching hour. That's right. *That's right*, my little guy."

He wails.He's just learned to crawl and is doing it now—sluggishly, from one end of his crib to the other. She senses Paul behind her, stumbling. "Closet," she says to him.

"Huh?"

"Check the closet."

While Paul does this she reaches down, scoops Theo up not by the arms or the armpits but *always*, the baby books tell her, the sides. Then holding him into her night-breasts a moment, just long enough to promise something, she rotates him into a perch on her forearm while nuzzling the hair on his little clay head. "Hungry or cranky or both? Both, huh? I'm *hankry*, mom, get with it—God!"

"There's nothing," says Paul.

"The crib," she says.

"There're blankets," he says.

"Underneath it."

"The floor."

"Paul."

"Okay, okay," he says.

"I've got him here."

"Okay," he says.

He squats, and huffs, and pokes his head. Then he wiggles his ass and emerges once more. "Like I said, the floor," he says.

He rises and bows in a satire of gallantry. His pajama pants are printed with a grinning carton monkey. "A woman's voice, I swear," she says.

The baby's screaming in her ear.

"A woman saying what?" says Paul. Even though Theo can't speak human yet, Moira gestures at her husband: a cross between hang-loose and off-with-his-head. Moira doesn't want Theo to hear Paul say "woman." But she just said "woman." Their fight makes no sense.

"Well I can't do anything right, can I, Moira?"

"This. Is. Not. About. You, Paul."

Paul answers, "Exactly," as Theo's pitch changes, ratcheting into skill-saw mode, so Moira strikes out for the old rocking chair donated by some family member, the patterns she's rubbing in Theo's tensed back growing tighter and tighter the nearer she draws. "My little demented baby man. Inconsolable woes he must suffer!" says Moira.

She sits in the chair now, which faces the window, which frames the semi-urban street and starts to rock Theo while freeing a nipple, remembering the woman's voice.

"Daddy's a martyr but Daddy's all right. Isn't he, mister psycho ward? We love daddy for who he is." Her milk lets down. She takes a breath. Her head is clearer in these moments before the feeding fog sets in and she feels—*call her cheesy, whatever, she feels it!*—that the scales of the cosmos have tipped in her favor.

Her husband stands there at her side, massaging her neck as she breastfeeds their son.

"Couldn't get back to sleep last night. So I did a little research," says Paul over breakfast.

"What did you find?" Moira says, pecking yogurt, surprised to hear she still knows words after so little sleep in her infant son's room. Moira's mind is dull with worry. Or maybe fuzzy is the word—with worry and feeding her eighteen-month-old more often and longer than probably she should. Indeed, some days the feeling is so heavy on her she feels she can't go one more step, as though she is two people, both Moiras, both tired, one of whom sleeps at the drop of a hat while the other is vaguely concerned for this person: uncouth narcoleptic who wanders the house.

Theo's with her even now, ensconced in her under-neck/clavicle region like she's some kind of beanbag chair, which makes it hard to eat her yogurt. Calmly and reasonably spooning in Puffins, her husband sits across the table. "Saleswoman told us, remember?" says Paul. "Trying to move the better model."

"So the monitor's to blame?" says Moira.

"The monitor, yeah," Paul explains, "and the Trotters. You know, the Trotters, three doors down?"

"Christiane Trotter," she says, nodding vaguely, rolling her neighbor's name inside her mouth.

"It's like in that movie? The guys on the train? What is it that they say? Criss-cross. The monitor frequencies cross," says Paul while knitting the air above his toast, "and she hears you with Theo, here, and you hear her, out there, with—um…"

Paul briskly snaps his fingers at her, summoning the baby's name.

"Gina," Moira answers for him and Paul settles back, satisfied with himself while Theo headbutts Moira's chin. Last week when they'd purchased the new baby monitor, Paul had wanted to get the better model, but Moira had opted for the cheap one, perhaps not wanting to acknowledge that they needed to keep such a close eye on Theo after only just starting to loosen their watch. "Oh," says Moira. "*Ohhhhhh*," she says.

But in her mind she says: *Perhaps.*

Is it strange Paul has referenced a film about murder, Hitchcock's

Strangers on a Train, to clear up what happened to Moira last night? He might've opted for a romcom—a meet-cute where two single parents cross signals, end up in each other's lives. But no, Paul has referenced a film about murder, where men not overfond of women decide to swap murders to look less suspicious, the exact sort of narrative Paul shouldn't mention (a) after last night, and (b) to his own wife, though this isn't exactly atypical of him. He doesn't always read the room. He likes to explain certain concepts directly and certain metaphors are best.

The work that Paul does has to do with computers. Yes, something to do with refurbishing code or something to do with protecting its function, or in any case something her mind never grips for long enough to see it whole—and not because Moira does not understand it. To hear the things Paul does all day is like watching mute frames in a used-car commercial, with the mind slipping off, glomming on, always slipping. He'd been elegant at explaining it once on a night in the year just before they were married having takeout and wine on their living room floor, elaborating how computers, these things that they used, these things that they depended on operated like obsessive compulsives at home. Such a person, Paul said, if set down in a room—let's say, to find a hair curler—would hunt among the objects there, making keen algorithmic assessments of each to determine if each of them wasn't the curler but of course at these massive accelerant rates that far outstripped the human mind. To demonstrate for her, Paul had put down his wineglass, pretended to lose it, then find it again.

Moira had liked the efficiency of it—the poetic efficiency, sure, why not. It was nothing to do with computers themselves, it had been Paul's description of them.

Now, too efficient, Paul tells her, "You've got this. This is nothing compared to…" Paul trails off. She can tell he doesn't want to say it, the name of Theo's prolonged illness that has only just settled, their whole life scorched by it. "We've got this, together," Paul tells her. "Just us."

He says it with bluster and sweetly. He is.

Paul comes to stand above her chair. Takes the bowl and the spoon from her hands, sets them down. Then he wraps his arms tightly around her and Theo, who's fooling around in Moira's hair. At first it's a little too tight. Moira squirms. Then it starts to feel okay.

Later that morning with Theo conked out, Moira has households that she could be doing.

The laundry. The dishes. The food-crusted tiles. Emailing her sister, grand-tragic in love. Speaking to the neighbor woman with the monitor signal that crosses with hers. Trying to get to the bottom of that which still carrion-pecks at her mind with unease.

It isn't that Paul's explanation is thin. What her husband Paul said makes exorbitant sense (*too much goddamned sense*, thinks Moira) and ever since Theo's unspeakable illness she's turned her back on sense, as such. So she wants something, mainly, to sharpen her mind so Moira can cut to the core of the mystery lying under the one Paul has already solved. It's a capable mind, she knows— *believes*. Just a little fuzzy lately. She needs something to, sort of, jar it. So she sits down in front of the monitor's speakers, scans through the dial for some good, solid static, and scribbles free-hand with the sound in her ears, remembering the woman's voice.

This is not a dream journal, it wasn't a dream. It's not strictly a record, either. *Automatic*, the words just come up in her, *writing*. What the Spiritualist mediums used to do to contact those beyond the veil, but mostly it will be a story—the story of the woman's voice.

Yet all that comes to mind are scenes. Or cuts, rather, from scenes from films but divorced from their titles, their narrative structures. The films are shrill ones, midnight chillers. In them, people mostly die. Yet they'd been Moira's happy place through the long predawn torpors of Theo's first feedings or in the months after when he'd gotten sick—when he had lain there, lolling, weak, his skin a hash of flaking redness. The Juvenile-Derma-something-something could be combatted several ways (vitamin supplements, antibiotics, topical ointments with byzantine labels) but the very best way, they had told her, was her: the rest and the healing she brought with her milk. And so just when she thought she'd be freer of nursing, she found herself back in the stranglehold of it. The sprawling and listing, the hourly engorgements. The back-pain and nipple-chafe making her wild. She'd watched the movies on her laptop with Theo strapped suckling over her middle, jump-cuts from the screen flashing onto his cheek. A lot of the doctors and books said no screen-time, even indirect screen-time before they turned two, but Moira kept the volume down, the computer itself balanced over her knees. She would sit through the movies, absorbing them, almost. Their creeping ambience—their death. Their gloom and their agony humming in her, they would succor her soul as she succored her son. She would say to Paul, "Guess what I watched with the baby!"

And Paul would say, "Don't—" before catching himself.And then he would say, "Watch whatever you want."

34

A door creaking open in front of a candle. A rocking chair rocking with nobody in it. A pair of hands laving off blood in a sink. A woman descending in only a nightgown from some darkness-kept and vertiginous height. A body splayed prone at the bottom of stairs. A strap for restraining extended and drawn.

She writes: I wake at three a.m. from a series of plodding and linear dreams to the voice of a woman not myself speaking over the snow of my son Theo's monitor. ~~The voice says~~… [She pauses, considers, redacts.] ~~The voice says~~… [She musses the monitor's dials.] ~~The voice says~~… [She taps the blank page, hearing static.] ~~The voice says~~… [She writes it again. Then again.]

That night, she hears the voice again.

It says: "… thee … art … strahlbam … mmky…. weeurt … eeurt … ehuhu … gratch … aaarfink … mmm … theaaarfink … aaarmpir … evaan … tadriiin … eelthas … rrrate …"

"Don't," says Paul.

He churns his limbs. But Moira, who's already risen, ignores him. "You're kidding me."

"Just don't," he says. "Oh go ahead." He flops and snorts.

Not the snort of a man but machinery, stalling, and Moira says to him: "My round?"

In the morning Paul goes to his hair-curler job so it makes sense that Moira is getting up now, though when she goes in to calm Theo at night, the child can smell the milk in her. If Paul

went in, Moira has said, then Theo might go back to sleep without feeding. But every night their son wakes up and Paul never
seems to remember their talk. "Remember, the Trotters," he says.
"Christiane," as though to calm Moira without getting up.

But to Moira it sounds like: *remember the Trotters*.

And stumbling this time down the hall, she brings the monitor along, while the beams from its lights, very red in the dark, go
projecting out into the not-space before her. The picture frames, the
attic rope, the cold blackened square of the uppermost landing, the
baby gate stamped, in long channels, across it. *The stairs*, she thinks,
are to the right. The woman's voice begins to dwindle. "… theaaarfink …. aaarmpir … evaan …"

And tucking the monitor under her arm, she enters Theo's still-
dark room.

The signal is clearer than ever in here with the transmitter/
receiver so close to each other and she can hear her own footsteps
as she walks to the crib of her son and looks in.

Not a lot happening with Theo, she sees, who is only just
coming awake on his back. She checks in the closet, then under the
crib, the same sequence as Paul before. All the while her son coos
faintly. But when Moira leans over his crib in distress, the darkness
erupts with a hideous wail.

Social mirroring, she thinks. She does not look how she should
look. And she feels she has failed him, just so, in that instant, it's
a deeming-unfit by a million small cuts. "Theo, sweetheart," Moira
says. "What's the problem, sweetie, huh? Where does it hurt? *Does
it hurt? Are you hungry?*" Moira inspects him top to bottom, sees
it is the latter case. "Hungry," she says half to him, half to Paul,
though already she knows that Paul can't hear her. She says it with
a slack contempt. As in, *You come in here and whip out your tit*.

After breastfeeding Theo for thirty-five minutes, then singing to him with her hand on his back, she returns to their room with the monitor buzzing. Theo seems quiet. She ratchets the volume. The snowstorm wakes Paul up again: a moan, then a lift and a drop of the head. "I heard the voice again," she says. "I'm sleeping in his room tonight."

And having informed him is turning to leave when Paul says something to her, muffled. "Rrrrgtllll," he says. She stops. Her husband's voice sounds like the voice of the woman.

"I can't hear what you're saying, Paul."

"Digital." His voice comes clear as he lifts his face out of a mountain of pillows. "Newer model—Jesus, Moira. Bought one today on my way home from work."

When Paul says that, he sounds so angry. Momentarily, Moira's too stunned to respond. It's an anger that feels disproportionate, really, to anything she's asking of him. Even if she's being silly, her silliness seems like the serious kind. Normally, she'd be annoyed— hell, even pissed, she'd let him have it. But right now for some reason in the dark of their bedroom with the strange woman's voice dwindling on the air, Paul's reaction confuses her. Frightens her, even. Makes her question: *is it Paul?* Almost like a different man who isn't her husband has zipped on his skin and is now lying there in this Paul-husband costume, irate at being woken up. "You bought one? You *had* one?" she says.

But Paul's silent.

The monitor placates Moira: *Shhhhh.*

A night-forest parting in front of two hands. A cat with its whiskers electrified, hissing. A penitent figure turned into a corner. A maul being dragged on a floor, trailing sparks. A young woman walking through sere autumn streets who glances back once, then again, sensing something.

She writes: I heard the voice again. [She crosses it out, waits a beat, and rewrites it] It isn't my voice but it might be—it isn't. [~~It might be~~ she begins to write] ~~I sit up in bed to endure from the speaker the first in a series of seething warped waves.~~ It says: ... thee ... art ... strahlbam ... [She pauses] ... mmky ... weeurt ... ehu ... aarfink ...

After dinner, Paul sets up the *rrrrgtlll* monitor.

As he assesses power strips, follows long chords to their terminal hardware, and enters a series of passwords and codes to be sure everything is "synced," Moira watches him throughout, the baby churning in her arms. She kind of wants to ask the whiz if he's sure he knows what he's doing this time. Partly to razz him like she likes to do, but also partly to be sure that the man on the floor on all fours is her husband, remembering the other Paul who only showed his face last night. This digital model is silver and sleeker—less rabbity-looking in the light and less demonic in the dark. It even has, on Moira's end, a video feed that records for close viewing.

Moira does not like this feature—even though she knows she should. The witching-hour temptation of it is going to incur on her massively, nights.

And then, at last, it's time for bed. First the baby's, then their own.

She feels it scrolling under her like a rag of loose earth at the edge of a cliff. Or like the fear of certain death that Moira would feel as a girl, before flying.

Tomorrow, I'm going to die, she'd think. *They call it air travel, but really, they're wrong. When I wake in the morning tomorrow,* she'd think, *it's the last time I'll ever wake up on this earth.*

"Wadda ... sheee ... duuu... tayo ... thee ... whadda ... shee ... du ... deedur ... bewe ... meurrt ... eee ... sarrright ... sssss ... okii ...

Moira wakes up. Moira always wakes up. The world is keeping secrets from her.

She engages the eye of the video feed, but she's not ready yet. So she switches it off. The digital monitor blathers and warps. Her heartbeat swallows at the room—at everything near to her, vast and aggressive. She presses the video button again and the image resolves in a black-and-white grain, bending in and out of true like a body is seizing beyond the transmission. Moira takes a little while to recognize the room that comes: the boxy shape of Theo's crib and the rest of the room narrowing toward the door.

Casually, almost, a figure blurs past.

The voice continues: "Wadda ... sheee ... duuu ... tayo ... thee ... o ... eee ... sarrright ... sssss ... okii ... trrrr ..."

And the figure, it crosses the feed-frame again but this time in a sort of circle, stalking along the top edge of the crib with its back to the lens. The figure has hair that's as long as her own and possibly as dark as well, though Moira can't be sure of it given the camera's impure resolution.

She thinks to wake Paul again—thinks to, but doesn't. Doesn't want to be furious he won't believe her, especially now that the woman bends down with her Moira-esque hair falling over her shoulders, lifts their son from where he lies and turns her face into the lens. The woman is Moira. Not like her, but her.

Moira here and there, she thinks.

And yet there's something very wrong with the size and the shape and the tone of her eyes. The eyes are dark and pupil-less, two sloppy ovals spaced apart—and yet they do not seem organic to the surface of the skin around them. They look drawn on, this Moira's eyes. Or rather scribbled on and depthless. As though underneath them a canvas of skin had been stretched, for detailing, between Moira's temples. And then the figure turns around and carries Theo toward the door, and as it goes the figure bends while at the same time growing smaller until the swaying of the gown is visible inside the frame.

Just what is she looking at there? It's a tail.

She can't tell if it's furred or not. Or leathery or even wooden. But sure enough it lifts the nightgown, stirs the air above the floor.

Moira bolts from the side of her bed. She's off running. Pictures, railing, deep dark drop. The stairs are always to the right. The baby gate is always locked.

But when she enters Theo's room and hammers on the lights above him, the woman is nowhere. Her Theo is sleeping. Her son is sleeping on his back with one of his arms out-flung behind him, as though with plans to throw something the moment that he comes awake. His face is calm and inward-turned, with the pruney and guru-like aspect of infants, but Moira cannot help herself: she leans inside and picks him up.

"What did she do to you? What did she do? Did the bad lady hurt you? It's all right. It's okay."

He wakes up peacefully this time. His face registers just the slightest bemusement. While Moira, in frenzy, turns in on herself, whirling around Theo's room like a nut.

Holding him, she checks the closet. Holding him, she checks the bed. And holding him closer to her ever more she stands above the rocking chair, getting lost, as she does, in the weave of the seat, in the secretive grain of the grid of it, coursing. She has slept in that chair in one form or another for the last ten consecutive nights, she thinks now. But it is strange to see it there—to see the chair without her in it. As though maybe it only and truly exists when the seat of it presses the backs of her thighs.

The next morning comes.

She feels chafed, hollowed-out. She does not say a word to Paul. Now not because he won't believe her (he would have to believe her by now, wouldn't he?) or because she's still scared of the strange, angry Paul who came awake the other night, but rather because Moira doesn't want Paul to go dredging about in her signature mystery.

One question being, how the woman. Another, why the woman comes.

She lets him, then, enjoy his food. In fact, she goes and makes it for him.

She takes out the organic eggs and she cracks three of them on the rim of the bowl and when their insides slither forth and stretch thinly into the bowl, the flattened yellow pouches of them remind her of the woman's eyes. She scrambles them noisily, not looking up.

Her husband, meanwhile, is communing with Theo. He's the dad-of-the-goddamn-decade overnight. "What's good in baby-land today? Do you have any baby appointments?" says Paul. Theo makes a moaning sound. "Maybe a baby board meeting?" he says. "I hope you're on the baby phone-tree. That way they can reach you in case it gets canceled."

This one really tickles Theo. He makes the moaning sound three times, ascending on the final one and Paul responds, "You're on it, huh? But does baby-HR have your name in their records?"

Moira doesn't see in time the stove is up too hot for eggs and the sliding morass of gelatinous orange touches down in the pan and dispels upon contact, blooming across with crusty runs. Her husband and son turn their heads at the sound. A vista of loneliness opens in Moira. "Baby alarm-bells, huh, big guy? Adult alarm-bells, too," says Paul.

After Paul heads off to work, Moira takes stock of the digital model.

Theo's on the kitchen floor so nothing comes over the feed but his bedroom—the fish mobile, the empty crib—but Moira presses random buttons. The video-feed changes qualities, colors. She finds that she can freeze the frame. The audio-feed comes in clearer, sometimes, when the video-feed is not turned on. And then Moira presses a series of buttons in a sequence that she can't recall. The feed adjusts its provenance to what appears to be last night: the woman, her back to the monitor's lens, leaning over the crib of her son to abduct him.

Moira hits the pause button. Clearly, there has been recording.

In the time signature in the bottom left corner, she sees there is only the slightest delay between when the woman walks out holding Theo and when she enters in her gown. She thinks it is remarkable, how much she resembles this woman of prey, her eyes redacted from her head. How much she resembles this woman who walks before the brushing of a tail.

Between when the woman walks out of the room and when she enters from the hall, the deficit is fifty seconds. This accounts for the time she'd been lost in the hall without a channel to her son—the cognitive dead-zone that in Moira's mind is so much more than just a hall. But when she got to him, her son was asleep. Her son was asleep on his back and unharmed. She checks the time-lapse, double-checks it. Plays it with the sound up loud. "What did she do to you? What did she do? Did the bad lady hurt you?" And Theo starts crying.

She rewinds to the moment that pulled her from sleep, with the blathering words coming over the wireless. "Wadda … sheee … duuu … tayo … thee … whadda … shee … du … deedur … bewe …"

The woman's words are Moira's words, delayed and slowed down by that same fifty seconds. It's the sound of her voice from some weird, occult record. Her voice though a syrup of horse tranquilizers.

Sometime over the course of her investigations, her son's made it into the Tupperware drawer. He sits in a pile of old wonton soup cartons, scraping plastic over tile.

A dollhouse in darkness save circles of eyes. A monkey with cymbals performing a dirge. A woman in a foul nightgown, lurching through a churchyard, grasping.

I wake up, she writes. ~~But~~ I always wake up. [She bores at the page with the tip of her pencil] The world is keeping secrets from… [She writes her name, redacts] ~~From who?~~ Moira, she writes, then redacts. ~~Or not Moira.~~ I am not ready yet. So I switch it ~~to~~ off. It is Christiane Trotter… [She thinks, pencil poised. She gnaws at the edge of the instrument, hungry]

" … frrrk … ink … vistrrrg … yaaalll … beesh … frrrk …"

Moira doesn't wake up. Moira hasn't been sleeping. She sits up calmly in her bed.

In the light of the LED display, which now shows green instead of red, Moira sees the dead black screen of the video feed, its on-button below it. Though she could've not done it, she presses it on. The epileptic image blooms, and the audio-feed struggles through a brief fritz, and Moira waits to feel as fixed as the camera that brings her the picture that comes: the woman with the long dark hair and the light, high-backed nightgown, bent over the crib, but this time on the other side so that her face is turned toward Moira with her hair fallen over it, hiding her features.

She appears to be missing her arms to the elbow. They're reaching into Theo's crib. And then the arms are drawing up, the dark hair is parting, the woman, she lengthens, this woman who bends but also grows, and her strange face appears to grow out of her hair like a knot in a tree under time-lapse surveillance. The eyes are depthless, scribbled black. The arms are all there and they're cradling Theo. Moira's been fixed to the spot all this time but now Moira's mobile. She's going, she's running.

The dead space of the hall—what is it?

A moment in time, Moira thinks, then redacts. A part of a structure amid other structures. A medium, like air or ink, that contains no beginning or end as we know them, but is in itself a containment of sorts that adapts its dimensions to what it has in it.

The picture frames, the attic pull, the drop of the stairs into nothing at all, the baby gate askew, somewhat or is the hallway bending, too, and Moira's vantage heals, corrects, the moment she comes out the other side of it.

The woman who bends over Theo is gone. The bed, the closet. Theo's fine. "Fucking tagalong bitch. Fucking coward," says Moira.

So she traces her steps to the door, through the hall and soon she is back on the side of her bed. She engages the camera. The woman is back, appropriating Moira's words. "Yeer … bissshh … erf … eeyer … bissshh … erm … rrrr … hew … dedoo … rrrl … ket … sew … seeze …"

Then rising up on one pale leg, the woman begins to hop in place. Her tail lifts the hem of her nightgown behind her. She stares at the camera, no joy in her face, just a straining and ludicrous look of commitment.

Moira laughs. Her husband stirs.

Her husband Paul who's there beside her, not asleep but in sleep-mode, recharging his guts. He shoots up like a crash-test dummy and reaches for Moira. He catches her wrist. "Don't go, now, *don't*. Goddamn it, Moira!"

The other Paul is back again. He gradually tightens his grip until—pain. She tries harder to free herself, whimpering faintly so real-Paul will hear her, corkscrewing her arm in the vise of his grip while the other-Paul stares at her, white in the eyes. The pain is great now, panic-worthy. Other-Paul's going to leave a bruise. And though on some level she is terrified of the man who is not and yet still is her husband, it's never to the same degree that she is of the not-Moira down the dark hall and the surge of it lets Moira jerk her wrist free. She cradles the wrist as she runs from the room. Yet when she arrives short of breath back in Theo's, the woman who bends is (predictably?) gone. But she has left for Moira traces, or are they forebodings of when she was there. Moira starts to hop in place while staring at the camera's eye.

Why am I hopping? she thinks to herself.

"To be sure that *she* hops," she says.

To be sure that the woman who bends has been hopping a full fifty seconds ago in real time.

At some point, she leaves Theo's room, bound for hers.

While at some point, she turns the receiver off, on.

While at some point, she's drawn to the transmitter lens where the eyes of the woman who bends are forthcoming and bending down to see herself she places her son, absently, on the floor.

While at some point, she tugs at the hem of her gown.

While at some point, she claws through her night-hair, one-handed.

While at some point, she runs down the hallway again to always just miss crossing paths with the woman, this woman with black eyes, this woman who bends.

While at some point, running down the hall for what seems like the thousandth time, Moira crosses paths with Theo, crawling unsteady and unsupervised and passing under Moira's legs.

While at some point, she's back on her side of the bed, locking eyes with the eyes of the woman without them and the woman who is but is not her, she stares at Moira down the feed.

And the face Moira sees, suddenly, is afraid. It is concerned, at any rate. Yes, the face of the woman appears to see Moira despite its lack of seeing organs and doesn't seem to like her face—maybe finds her, or not-her, if they are both Moira, an all too real and present threat, and before Moira runs down the dark of the hall where Theo's gate is swinging open, she briefly wonders to herself if the woman who bends isn't watching her, too, in her own restless bed, with her husband beside her, awaiting the moment when Moira bends down, her mysterious hair failing over her shoulders.

SKIN OF VELVET, BUDS LIKE SNOW

Before the California earthquake of 1906—twenty-three hours before it exactly—a quake which will, when it has passed, enact such a chaos of structural damage upon a house in San Jose that the house might as well not be standing at all, shattering ten of the seventeen chimneys, shaking the three Tudor turrets to bricks, uprooting a wing of New England-style porches, collapsing the seven-tier tower to dust—before any of this, while the house is still standing, while the house is still pumping with uncanny blood, Sarah Winchester, the woman who owns it, proceeds through its windings with Tommie her gardener, counting each and every window.

Rooms in the house: one hundred and sixty.

Forty-eight fireplaces. Seventeen chimneys. Three elevators. Two basements. Two ballrooms. At least ten thousand panes of glass.

Only some of these windows look out on the gardens where Tommie, cadaverous and elegant, walks. While other windows in the house look sideways at walls or look upwards on ceilings. They are curious windows, interior windows. Rather than leading outside, they lead inward. A couple look through dim woodwork upon still other windows and through these the gardens. Between some windows lies a shaft with no architecture above or below it, an extra dimension of vertical space encasing the house like some strange second skin.

Every glass pane counts as one discrete window. The heiress, Lady Winchester, has made sure of this. Even the stained glass surmounting the staircase which cost one thousand dollars and took two weeks to install goes down in Tommie's book as one—one mark among a legion like it. The glass has an inscription on it from Richard II, Act V, Scene V:

These same thoughts people this little world.

She is an heiress but also a widow. Her daughter is four decades dead, her husband three. She is alone. The heiress' fortune comes to her from rifles—the Winchester model, named after her husband, who carries the name of his father in turn. But she is the primary shareholder now. She owns the house and never leaves it. And now every two weeks she goes hobbling through it, calculating what she's built.

She and Tommie come into the house's ballroom where she turns in a circle; the dust motes turn with her. All the curtains are drawn in this cavernous space. Daylight filters through the cracks. "Seven thousand four hundred and twenty-six, Tommie."

Tommie marks inside his book. "Are we counting the panes in the greenhouse today?"

"Of course, Tommie, yes," says the heiress, distracted, ticking off panes with her right pointer finger. Chronic arthritis sets fire to her hands, bringing her back to the moment—his question. She turns and arranges her face into sternness. "Of course we are. Why would we not?"

To reach the east staircase that leaves the ground floor and winds into the upper stories, they'll have to double back again down the hall that led here, then the hall at the branching, then a series of shorter halls still off of that—a kinked-up maze of passages that leads to the alcove that houses the stairs. There are many staircases all through the great house, though few of them lead to the places they should. Like the windows, the stairways melt up into ceilings or end mid-ascent in bizarre, floating platforms. They have a purpose in the world that they've been divested of here in the house.

"Tomorrow is Wednesday," says Tommie.

"Which means?"

"A good day for a holiday."

"Of course, you may take the day off," says the heiress. "Spend it with Ito, your pretty young wife."

"It's not on my..." The gardener stops. "It's not on my *behalf* I ask."

She echoes him, "On my behalf." And then she smiles. "That's lovely, Tommie."

She is happy Tommie has a wife who misses him when he is here helping her. She is happy Tommie has two children—a boy, just turned two, and a girl, almost eight, though the heiress prefers not to talk about them unless, like today, she is strictly obliged. She decides she's happiest of all that Tommie's English is improving. Perhaps the Radcliff, better yet the Flaubert—the Blaydes translation, the heiress insisted. She has given him so many books in the past, stacked them outside his quarters, not insisting he read them. She wants to rid Tommie of halts in his speech, the sharp falls of his Japanese. Only then, she is certain, will others treat Tommie as they are too terrified not to treat her—at least when she's in hearing distance.

Tommie's figure is vague through the heiress' veil, which is crepe and gusts out with the air of her motion, approaching him, passing him, leaving the room. She only removes it when she bathes and when she is in bed asleep. Tommie has seen her without it, of course, but she prefers to keep it drawn. Beneath it is not even something macabre: the necrotic grand dame with the straggling hair. It is only the face of an elderly woman who cannot fully chew her food.

The heiress tinkers in the greenhouse.

Her shadow is visible, crossing the panes: her veil and the stiff tailoring of her dress like a jellyfish floating through labyrinths of coral. You might think that given the shadow of Tommie preceding the heiress' through the high gloom, and given the way that they move in the windows, gliding and pausing and stooping and rising, that they're busy including the greenhouse's panes in the heiress' weekly master-count, but they're there on a gentler, more private errand. A third shadow of many arms and taller than Tommie's waits for them mid-room and they circle around it in worshipful poses.

The heiress kneels and bows her head.

The heiress is due in the house's grand parlor where Samuel Leib, her lawyer, waits.

After the greenhouse with Tommie she goes there, the cherry buds thick as a balm on her hands and Leib has been sitting in decorous humor with his downturned mustaches, in coat and cravat. It might be mid-evening for all there is light and the hearth is dull-seeming with smoke through the irons. The day in the garden hangs drizzly and cold. The fire that burns for Leib is Tommie's and so it is a famished fire, for Tommie has never liked Leib and distrusts him, though he has been to her a trustworthy counselor and even along the far margins a friend.

She takes the chair across from Leib, who says, "He is a crafty man."

Leib might be but isn't referring to Tommie, who stands in the shadows just right of the fire, recording the words that they say in his daybook between window counts of the last several months so she can read them later on and ponder if she has been wise. The heiress frowns and smooths her skirts. "You did not strike a deal with him?"

"His game was entrapment. There's no guessing that."

"But you came back retaining a part of the sum?"

"I have half of it here in my pocket," says Leib.

"And what should I do with this face?" says the heiress. But she does not remove her veil.

"You are," says Leib, "a lovely woman."

The lawyer says this all the time. He is a sort of husband, then, with whom she does not share her bed. "It is the principle, I think. I ordered up dentures, he didn't fulfill them."

"The teeth are mere utility. You will manage with no teeth and still have your smile."

It had been just a tooth at first, a top-left incisor that spiked on the porcelain while Sarah was standing there scrubbing her gums. Graceful as a suicide it had leapt from her mouth to the basin below her. She had held it before her, intractable, bloodless, peered into her ruined gum. Raw and hollow of her tooth, it had looked like the pupa of something newborn. After that she and Tommie had hired out a dentist, a slick San Franciscan who'd come recommended, but he had botched the job and well. The dentures did not even fit her.

"Other things," Leib says, "are brewing."

"Financial other things?" she says.

The lawyer nods. "If I am here."

"My will," she says, "paid out in bullets."

"I will transcribe it, if that is your wish. Channel it in your best interests."

"And what are my interests?" she says, leaning forward and cupping her chin in the palm of her hand.

"To relinquish your stocks to the interested parties. To claim your share and step aside. They are tired altogether of whether you're well. They want their stake or they want out."

"And you have advised them what course?" says the heiress.

Leib smiles at her forbearingly. "To calm their wits or lose their shares."

"You are good to me, Samuel. Thank you."

"I have tried."

Tommie closes his daybook and moves from the gloom. He comes to stir the fireplace. "You build and build and build," says Leib. "And yet you leave nothing for what happens next."

She tells the lawyer, "Spinsterhood. I would venture to say it is already here."

"Your legacy, I mean," says Leib.

"My legacy, really?"

The heiress is tired. Tired of guns, tired of lawyers. All the men she's ever known rhapsodize about guns, their mechanical grace, but she hates them and always has. Every several years or so she endeavors this same conversation with Leib concerning the prospects of interested buyers who would ferry the awfulness out of her hands and every couple years or so the heiress demurs, then retreats through her maze. She marvels Leib still humors her; she marvels he is here at all. She will not sell the company. Not this year and not the next.

"You have always been generous with me," says Leib. "I hope I have not made offense. I am telling you, Sarah, my office apart, that you must sometimes plan ahead."

"I was planning ahead with those dentures," she says and looks at the fire for a time, back at Leib.

She has ordered that work on the house never cease, in nighttime and daytime, in sun and in rain. The pounding and grinding, the groaning and sawing, goes on at all times of the dark and the day—though less so in the night, of course, when the workers are prone to committing mistakes that have injured a couple of them, but no deaths.

On days she travels through the house with her veil hanging over her wrecked, toothless face, she has heard them discussing her, architects, builders, her chief architect, a man named Denan, in little cabals of man-spite, beneath scaffolds: "She could no more imagine a building, that woman, than conjure a husband to suffer her touch."

Though they are awful, they are right. The heiress' eye is completely untrained, and the house is paean to botched architecture.

Denan is the heiress' chief architect because Denan is building-savvy, though all of the major decisions are hers—each window and staircase, each turret and shingle. The elements he ridicules are totems of her trial and error. Yet his ridicule ever goes only so far, the heiress has noted, and never on paydays.

On those days he says she is getting a knack. And sometimes the heiress will almost believe him.

All the money that comes from the selling of guns she pours into the house—its upkeep, its increase. There is seemingly, frighteningly, no end to money. The Winchester rifle, the heiress now knows, has done terrible things to the tribes of the West but she has weighed the consequence against the house and found it lacking. She'd even hired a medium to see if it would ease her guilt, but she had been an utter fraud.

So the heiress re-hired her, again and again.

The first time she'd had her come in through the kitchen so that her neighbors didn't see, and then when they were in the parlor, the heiress fed her sparingly: her husband, his handkerchief red in autumn, her daughter, dissolving away in her crib. When the heiress had mentioned the dead Indians the medium had asked her to please close her eyes. "The spirit that wishes to speak is no red man. The spirit that wishes to speak is a girl. A baby girl without a name. She is fresh from the belly. She is small and so thin. She is trying to keep something down to sustain her. Her mouth is chewing on the air. She is trying to live for you, mother, she says. She is trying to show you that she can withstand it, this malady that clouds her birth." At first she'd felt rage then a troubled acceptance: the little girl's name had been Annie Pardee. Unable to keep down her mother's sweet milk, she could not grow strong and had died of marasmus: uncomprehending agony in the new nursery at the top of the house. Yet now that grief weighed on her less every day, the heiress wanted to know more about her dead daughter. She was curious, almost, to hear her opinions, the kind of person she'd become, as though she were a full-grown woman returned to her mother from many years gone. "When you come calling over the cloud-banks to meet me," said the medium, grasping, beleaguered, absurd, "it is I who will come to the gates and admit you and I who will stand at the pass, and lead on."

From then on she'd have her come in through the front— always through the front, where the whole world could see. And the neighbors, her neighbors, would talk to their neighbors and those neighbors would talk to their neighbors in turn and a rosebush of madness would pulsate out from her, enclosing her behind its thorns. Her life was peaceful after that and the dishes and baskets were less at her door. The San Jose paper had published a headline: "Heiress Seeks the Spirits' Counsel."

Beneath the mansion's sleeping eyes, Lady Winchester steps out of her clothes.

While she soaks in the tub and chews willow bark scraps that she rubs on her feet and her hands once they're soft to lessen the pangs of her constant arthritis, Tommie flits about her bedroom, lighting the lanterns and blessing the bed. Done in the bathtub she rises by turns because she cannot rise at once, stretching her legs out and crooking her knees before fastening her hands on the sides of the tub and, with the mechanism set, she pushes herself gradually into sitting. She retrieves a hand towel from the edge of the sink. Gently, she spits up the chewed scrap of bark, a thin web of drool coming off of her gums. Her toothbrush is mottled with more and more blood; when she spits in the sink there is terrible pinkness. She gets in her nightdress and goes out to Tommie, who turns his eyes down when he sees her emerge. Then he locks, unlocks, and locks her door for a charm of three times before saying goodnight.

She wakes in the dark and the bed-frame is shaking.

It is, she thinks, the century's end before she remembers the date. Her heart falls. The bed appears to levitate, arising on its own vibrations and she is a caught up in it, hostage unto it, as it floats in the room before hunkering down. As soon as the legs hit, she springs out of bed. She has not moved this way in years. She is running, she thinks, to the door of the room where the lintel built into the wall will protect her, but just as she presses herself to the frame the ceiling behind her comes crumbling down.

She lies on her back staring up at raw beams. Flakes of cracked plaster rain down on her face. She does not need to go to the door of the room to know that she is trapped inside.

Most of the windows and mirrors have broken, inundating the room with a river of shards. She feels the gesture overtake her to record the smashed windows as three windows less. And that's when a sitting chair, ancient, brocaded, slides into the rift in the ceiling above her and hammers down upon its side just short of where she sits there, dazed. The heavy grooved arm of the chair cracks away and it skitters away to the wall; the rest settles. She rises and wraps herself up in her bedclothes and rights the smashed chair and sits down in it, tilted, and she cradles herself like a scared little girl. She reckons it is near to dawn by the way that light trembles upon the horizon. She raises a hand to the back of her head. It returns to her slick, amniotic with blood.

The earthquake's duration is forty-two seconds. Even so brief a time takes a terrible toll.

Looking north to San Francisco weird fires can be seen in the heart of downtown. And in spite of firebreaks to disable the blaze with dynamite and shell barrages, the separate fires become one conflagration, which blooms with appalling speed over the city. Three thousand people lose their lives. An enormous cache of botanical specimens, some newly discovered, are lost to the flames and the flag from the '46 Bear Flag Revolt, enshrined in the State Building, crinkles to ash. An opera singer come to town to play the tenor role in *Carmen* who absconds from the wreck of the Palace Hotel with a portrait of Roosevelt clutched in his hands vows never to visit the city again. San Jose does not catch fire, but the sundering force of the quake is enough. Not five miles from Llanada Villa, at the Agnew Asylum where lunatics dwell, hundreds are crushed when the cheap upper stories, like floors in a dollhouse, come tumbling down. Of the hundred or so who are not killed a good portion of them escape through the doors and the lunatics run through the night in their linens, unleashing their mad, strangled cries at the stars.

The clock in the sumptuous St. James Hotel stops dead at 5:13 a.m.

Hours seem to pass in the heiress' room.

Even the light appears to change: it is dawn, afternoon, eventide, dead of night. It might be the scattershot way the sun finds her, shining through the jagged glass then reflecting again off the puzzle-pieced mirrors which makes her feel that, in her room, she is moving too fast or too slow through the cosmos. Her vessel of selfhood has entered a doldrums. That, or a maelstrom which wheels her around.

She groans and she worries her hands, walking hunched. All is not well with the back of her head whose wetness she feels soaking into her collar.

She's seeking the Enunciator, set high and left of her bedroom's blocked door. It is carved in walnut with a clock centered in it and a sextet of brass knobs arrayed at the base. She has only to flutter the switch on the right and Tommie, if he is disposed, will come running. And yet when she presses the flat of the switch she hears only a lifeless clicking. She stumbles away from this useless convenience and sits where she stands—where she no longer can. The morass of the wrecked upper story juts upward, like the improvised ramparts of some revolution, and toward the middle of it all a baby grand's legs point down into the hole that used to be her bedroom ceiling. Every time the mansion shifts, the legs move closer to the edge.

The heiress decides she can't die here. She refuses to die like a child, beatific, with her atrophied legs folded up underneath her. She starts to crawl across the floor toward the part of the room that retains the most warmth—the worn escritoire where she writes when she can, centered in the eastern corner.

Her bedroom is freezing, her pain unrelenting.

The heiress says, "Uh," like a beast as she crawls. "Uh," she says—a few more feet.

And that's when the first of four aftershocks come, landing her hard in a sprawl on her stomach. The warped prominence of the house shakes above her, raining detritus upon the room's floor. All

her extremities soar with pain; the pain in her head is a comple-
ment only. And she realizes now, as she lies on the floor with the
last of the aftershocks settling around her, that she has never felt so
human, so kept by her flesh as she does at that instant.

To be human, she thinks to herself. *To be selfish.*

She cannot—will not—die like this, she'd never planned to die
at all. And suddenly the heiress sees that that is what she lacks:
a plan. Not a plan like Leib means, what to do with her money, but
why she builds and cannot stop, why she adds to the house when it
only reminds her of everything that she has lost. Yet now that the
house is a ruin around her and now that she reaches the base of her
desk, she sees that the greatest indignity yet would be to rebuild if
the house is destroyed. She sees it now as others see it: a haunted
place of fog and sighs, a superstitious woman's home who has built
labyrinths for the spirits that plague her—perhaps the same spirits,
she's heard in the papers, that her Winchester rifles have wiped
from this earth. To rebuild would be to admit she is mad on every-
body's else's terms.

In euphoria almost the heiress sits down and she coaxes a page
from the drawer on her desk. She dips her pen. She tests it, darkly.

She gathers the bedclothes in closer about her.

A third of her fortune she wills to her lawyer, another third yet
to her sister-in-law and still the last remaining third for what she
envisions as a specialty clinic which will treat, in her words, "pul-
monary unwellness and other afflictions of the chest." The house,
of course, she wills to Tommie. The proviso it not be rebuilt is
included. She makes Leib executor, lord of her shares—steward of
the corporation. The wrack-removal of the grounds she contracts
to Denan & Sons and leaves him, too, the prototype of a canon the
Winchester Arms Company had had manufactured for Sheridan's

army but never after reproduced—a big-bellied and snub-nosed thing that has sat for eight years in her furthest outbuilding and that Denan will have to haul by fits and starts to see it moved.

It would be no exaggeration to say that she throws back her head and she cackles. But the motion jogs something inside of her head. She sees the familiar expanse of her bedroom go swimming before her like something unmoored.

There are sounds in the house but she tries to keep writing. Her pen starts to founder. She dips it again. And then there comes a grating crash so near to her she can't ignore it. The door erupts inward, displacing the wreck. The forms of her lawyer and three other builders struggle clumsily over the reef that remains. She sees herself briefly as they four must see her: a feral spinster in a night-dress, bleeding from her very head, turning to herald her saviors with wildness, hunched above a cluttered page.

Now she looks at the will, but she can't recognize it. All she knows: it is for her. So she folds it and tucks it away in her dress as the men clear the wreckage and stand in the floor. "We are here, Mrs. Winchester, ma'am, to retrieve you."

"How many hours have I been here?" she says.

"Hours?" says her lawyer. And looks to the builders, one of whom consults his watch. "It has *not been* an hour," says Leib. "We came to retrieve you as soon as we could."

She has nothing to say to that—nothing at all.

And that's when her face hits the top of her desk.

How long she's lain here in her bed she cannot in good faith deter-mine. It's somewhere close to seven days and a couple of years, give or take. The light lengthens. It shines in her eyes and it heats up her face. There is a gauze upon her head, a splint and poultice on her nose.

My nose, she thinks, *no longer mine*. They tell her that now it belongs to her blotter. The piano poking through the ceiling has since been removed to elsewhere in the house, the rift in the ceiling provisionally patched, the mirror shards swept up and carted away. They advised her to leave the room at first before they realized she would not and now more than ever the heiress is conscious of living a life she has already lost.

Tommie is infrequent to her and mostly the lawyer comes there in his waistcoat. He enumerates for her all kinds of statistics that she can little understand, though she thinks it is mostly to do with the house and the infinite index of damage done to it and how to repair it will cost X, Y, Z. When she bothers to look out the window before her to catch a glimpse, perhaps, of Tommie, all that she sees are the slopes of her land tending up past her feet in a green-brown morass.

When the heiress is human again, Tommie comes. Light shines in her eyes. It must be early morning. What an elegant corpse is her Japanese gardener, with his long, frowning face and his stately dark eyes as he enters the room in his white linen suit.

She tries to rise. He frowns her down. "Are we feeling some better this morning?" he says.

"Oh rather ethereal, Tommie. This sun."

"They do not close the shade for you?"

"They seem to think I need the light."

She asks that Tommie leave her room so that she might dress for a turn in the garden and when he lingers Sarah tells him, wanting nothing so much as to dress by herself. The other reason being this: the process is going to lay torment upon her and she doesn't want Tommie to see her in pain.

Toward the back of the heiress' closet she finds it: a ruined nightdress, stained with blood. There are dirt smears and plaster smears on it as well, and they swirl with the blood like oil paints on a pallet. Tommie has probably left it there for her, not cleaned or destroyed, just to teach her a lesson. *This is what happens,* the ruined dress tells her, *to afflicted old women who take on too much.*

There is something outlined in the dress' front pocket.

She works her hand into the fabric and comes up with a folded page which by and by she picks apart to reveal what she sees is her own living will. And the will has provisos, recipients, clauses. It is, she reflects, a magnanimous will. There's a little dried blood in the will's top right corner. She has no memory of composing the thing—of writing it, signing it, bleeding upon it. Though that is the reason perhaps she does not: her head had smashed against her desk.

But this will that she holds in her hands, it delights her. It is so unexpected, so new—so unlike her. Even the part when she chastens Denan by bequeathing upon him her cumbersome canon is a fond, mordant gesture, a whimsical one.

And she thinks to herself: *well perhaps, then, I am.*

For the will in her hands is a treasure to her beyond even the measure of what it apportions. It deploys a strange energy, coursing, all through her. She should not—cannot—feel this good. She cycles briskly through her closet, flinging her dresses away on the rack and she comes upon one she has not worn in decades, a ridiculous dress of Victorian times with Mameluke sleeves and décolletage lace, and she binds herself up in its fanciful riddle of ruching and whalebone and zippers and stays. When the pain comes upon her—her fingers and wrists, her whiplashed neck and broken nose—the surge of delight that she feels overrides it. And she rides it, the surge, as she once did the pain. She rides it out into the hall, out to Tommie, whose arm she does not take at first on her way down a staircase that's partway caved in and has since been patched over with rudely cut boards; and she rides it down into the house's foyer where the Tiffany glass chandelier has been stripped, the vestige of its architecture casting shapes on the floor like a skeletal hand; and she rides it out into the garden at last where now she does take Tommie's arm, and as she moves beyond the house toward the yews and the hedgerows and the carven Demeter, she gazes up to see its ruin, her dream of ascension, of growth without end, reduced to a trimming of serrated edges. Her chimneys and turrets have crumbled and fallen. Her third and fourth stories are all but destroyed. Like a bible worn over her heart to a duel, the will is tucked inside her dress. And in spite of the puffy, bruised state of her face, she does not even wear her veil.

The heiress and Tommie aren't alone.

There are so many workers around them—too many. Men raking up rubble and picking up bricks and yanking down dreck from the hedges and trees, and dismantling aggregate, freestanding ruins of steel and stone and splintered wood. Not building the house, Sarah realizes now or even rebuilding it into its grandeur, but making it livable for her again. She wants to show the will to Tommie. It burns like an ember inside of her dress. She wants Tommie to know of course that he has been provided for but also that she has been wise, that she has heeded his advice and that the construction they now walk amidst on their way to the greenhouse that centers the maze is not a return to the past but a yielding. She wants him to know she has a plan.

With her arm hooked in Tommie's arm, they wend the sunny garden maze. It is a lovely April day—the sort that cannot, quite, be real. They are slow in their progress, the heiress and Tommie, under skies of sea-scented, unspeakable blue.

The side of the greenhouse comes up on the right, an ocean-liner all of glass. It is immense more so than most; fifteen hundred feet square, if the heiress remembers. When she'd first built the place fifteen years ago now she had always had Tommie in mind to care for it, all her sour-berry bushes, and daisies, and roses, and Indian hawthorn, and crepe myrtle blooms. But she notices now that some aspect is off.

The greenhouse is standing wrong, perhaps. It seems to be canted several yards to the left, and Tommie does not look at her as they round the front pathway and journey inside. "Is it different?" she says, just before the front entrance.

Inside, the April light refracts.

"I have been coming back," says Tommie, "for every day you were in bed."

What the heiress has hidden inside is not awful. What the heiress has hidden inside is her heart, beneath a cherry blossom tree that stands at the center of everything growing. Sarah's husband and daughter are under that tree, the roots of the tree twining over their leg-bones, the trunk of the tree jutting up in a mass from the concavity of the dead husband's ribs while Annie curls there in his arms, her head no bigger than his hand.

When she'd first disinterred and instated them here, how long ago she can't recall, her daughter was this little doll, two thumb-prints of darkness in place of her eyes. Her bones had knocked around her box, a precious nut inside its shell. Five times the stature of Annie Pardee and housed half as long in the grip of the earth, her husband had been only partway decayed and Tommie had had to prepare him with gloves in aligning his chest with the trunk of the tree. His spoliation year by year had mixed into the soil below him. The stronger scented flowers there had thinned though never masked the scent and the cherry tree grew with an unnatural vigor. Skin of velvet, buds like snow. Often in her daughter's skull there would collect at least three petals and if she watched them hard enough they would lend the illusion her soul had returned.

But when she arrives at the base of the tree she sees her kin have been disturbed.

The tree is uprooted. And its trunk has divided her husband in two when the tree-roots pulled free in the throes of quake. The upper part of him is shattered along with the body of Annie Pardee so that all that remains of the girl is her skull, where Sarah does not look for petals.

But Tommie has swept up the glass from the beds.

And Tommie has hauled the dead tree limbs away.

And Tommie has picked up her daughter and husband— a scapula, a shard of rib—and piled them up beneath the tree, a little pretty cairn of bones. Even the dirt-stained irregular bits that the heiress has trouble perceiving as human are shoring in her husband's trunk, her daughter's skull propped in the midst of his hipbones.

The earthquake had done this.

The earthquake, she thinks. As though to remind herself: *nature, not Tommie.*

The limbs of the tree appear black in the light. The cherry blossoms float and flash.

And then it is obvious to her, this life, and what she has intended by it—the reason she builds up her house without end and why she has kept herself hidden these years beyond her green labyrinth, her halls and staircases. It is simple and obvious, staring right at her: she has nourished the house as she could not her own. She has dwelt in the house as her dead dwell in her. But now that her family is lying in rubble beside the tree roots that supported their bones the widow Winchester sees no point at all in being magnanimous, wise, any of it. She sees no reason, in a phrase, to be anything more than she already is.

She is angry, she finds. Inconceivably so.

As angry now that she is here and she has seen what she has seen, as she was surprised and delighted before while her fingers unfolded the imbecile's will and she'd said to herself: *It is now I will face it. Finally I think I can.*

So it is simple for her, too, to let the vileness back inside and the heiress decides she will never stop building as she had planned to after all. She will rebuild the house and will build it the more beyond even the point of her death, which is coming and will visit the gall of her thwarted desires upon generations yet made in the earth so that not one of them will be able to say when they pass alongside of her ramparts and towers that here lived a woman who laid down for life.

They will know my name, she thinks. Or maybe she says it aloud. She's unsure.

Tommie is speaking to her—has been speaking. "The tree," he says, "it will grow back."

But already the heiress is mounting the planter. She is planting her feet, at great pain, in the sod. Not to cry or to worry her arthritic hands but to tear up the will that she has in her dress, the shreds of which she integrates by a sweep of her hand with the buds of the tree. "It's a pity, now isn't it, Tommie." she says. "Well, then." She breathes in. "What are we to do now?"

Sixteen years later the heiress will die on a day in September with Tommie beside her while the birds of the valley enliven the garden. Her mind will be utterly blank in that moment, not regretful or peaceful or spiteful at all, but maybe if only a little bit frightened to be leaving the earth as all people must do. And yet no single hammer-blow will mark the passing of the heiress—no death-knell punctuation sound, in the wake of which work on the mansion will cease, but the sounds of Denan and his men will continue and when Denan dies, Denan's sons and their sons. And when the house can grow no more, passed into the hands of executive parties only tepidly linked to the heiress by blood, the process will remake itself in outfitting the house as a roadside museum. And the road-side museum, along with the house, will pass through new seasons of glory and shame—at first a premier San Jose destination with well-informed docents and wall-text displays where the heiress' aura of mystery holds sway, and yet before long nothing more than a hovel, with bad circuit wiring and overpriced tours.

In this broken down spook house of piped-in laments, and eerie red lights that make phantoms of bureaus, and a carpeted gift-shop that peddles on racks postcards of the house in its dwindling gran-deur, one of the docents, locked in after hours and bleary from a day of drinking, will lose himself amid the halls that stretch and bend and double-back and increasingly panicked will run through the mansion, getting more and more tangled the further he runs, until, at the foot of the house's grand stairs, he will fumble his footing and fall to the landing.

The docent will survive this fall.

He will sprawl on the once-magisterial landing, laughing while nursing his twisted-up ankle and in his drunkenness will see or think that he sees for a moment no more the shade of a woman bent over with age, her face obscured by widow's weeds, going haggard and proud down the marble stairs slowly and into the garden in search of her heart.

But it's only the shadow of something outside as it tosses in fury beyond the dark glass. The docent will sit there a moment, recovering.

And when he is ready he'll hobble downstairs.

THE FLESH STRIP

When the daughter found the doll at The Salvation Army, she knew right away that her mother would love it.

The mother had always loved her dolls, perhaps more even than the daughter. But now that the mother was on her deathbed in the failing Victorian house they shared, her mind more occluded each day by dementia, there was little the daughter could see to deny her. Plus, the daughter preferred to think well of herself.

The daughter saw the doll's feet first, sticking out of the top of the bric-a-brac bin between the DVD rack and the kitchen appliances; there were tiny blue booties sewn onto the legs. They drew her in a forlorn way. When the daughter extracted the rest of the body she heard the sound of fabric, sucking. Head to toe it was roughly the size of an eggplant. The booties, hands, and head were porcelain; the torso matted, sticky cloth. The doll was filled with an impacted stuffing that had more in common with rubber than cotton, and the porcelain parts of it were shockingly heavy. If you swung it at someone, it would've done damage.

It was a kind of gnome, she thought.

Beneath this pointy hat-hood thing, the top of the head was melon-shaped, the bottom pink-cheeked and cherubic. Its eyes were sly, almost amused, glancing back at the daughter, the pupils tight-cornered. The nose, which took up a large part of the face, was bulbous and pig-like, its nostrils black. The red and upturned mouth smiled at her. Below it hung a wispy beard. Its clothes were, near as she could tell, a sort of alpine walking costume, grime-streaked and faded with handling and age. The texture made her fingers itch.

Something hidden in the hat pressed jaggedly against her palms. She had thought that the hat was sewn onto the head, but she flipped the brim up to reveal pointy ears. They were silly putty-colored, with intricate whorls. And now that the brim of the hat was pushed up, she felt something strange on the back of the neck. She tipped the doll down in the cup of her hands so the seat of its navy blue trousers faced towards her.

Between its ears a strip of pink ran across the back of the gnome-doll's neck. At first glance, she thought it was discoloration. A strip of pink paint where it should've been white. But no, it was more than that, subtly raised, separate from the neck itself, connecting the ears, a vestigial membrane. It had this wrinkly, slablike texture, like dried bubblegum slabbed over the porcelain.

Right away the words "flesh strip" came up in her mind, a series of words she had never combined or thought to combine in her years on this earth. No person or doll had anatomy like that. It was, she reasoned, some mistake, a dud in the assembly line, but something about it felt special, auspicious. Like a baby that's born with a caul on its face except here it was thick as an old keloid scar, horizontally spanning the back of the neck.

She brought the gnome-doll to the counter. "Nasty little fellow, ain't he?"

For years, the mother had been ill and the daughter had been her sole caretaker in the house where their family had clung on for decades in a small southern town at the edge of the Gulf.

The house was grey with purple trim and a burgundy, ginger-bread-style sloping roof. At one point in time it had looked stately, moneyed. But the subsequent decades had rendered it ragged. The wooden siding was dirt-streaked and scabbing off paint. The hurricane shutters hung on by a hinge, the bracketed porch columns blotchy with salt-stains. Damaged in last year's one-hundred-year-storm, the Witch's Cap was sloughing sideways. Jasmine and wisteria choked the front garden, strangely lovely from the road but only the daughter knew what lay behind it: an infection of night-shade, thick over the ground, climbing up the porch columns and onto the shingles.

To the daughter, the house was an asset, no more. It was hard to care how it might look to outsiders. And now that her mother made no sense at all, sifting and chanting odd jumbles of words ("Whimsy mimsy nimsy splat!") or reciting old songs she'd known as a girl ("Mary, Mary, Quite Contrary" or "Pat-a-Cake, Pat-a-Cake, Baker's Man"), the daughter supposed it mattered less. The mother's obsession with her dolls was a symptom of this same decline, something the mother had done as a girl that, just like the rhyming, was happening again the further the mother slipped away. The daughter encouraged it more than she should. But the mother had a wheelchair for trips through the house and a stair-lift for traveling up or downstairs, even if on most days when the daughter got home, the daughter would find her still lying in bed. The daughter had flirted with hiring somebody to tend to her mother while she was at work, but she had no insurance, the cost was too great. So

Tuesday through Sunday, when the daughter was working, shelving tinctures and ringing up loose marigold in the homeopathic health shop in the town she had only left twice in the course of her life—once to get an abortion when she was nineteen and once to see her favorite band in a dirty, hot city five counties away—the daughter changed the mother's diaper one time in the morning before going out and once in the evening before she retired, which usually happened between eight and nine. She left lunch, or what now passed for lunch, on the sideboard: cottage cheese, which would thicken and sour in the sunlight, or a deli-cheese sandwich with Heinz mustard on it. It was the least that she could do, never missing, to her recollection, one meal, even if the cottage cheese would only show a single gouge, the deli-cheese sandwiches nibbled and skewed like rats had been at them while she'd been asleep. It was no kind of life for either of them, but it would have to do for now.

Ideally not for very long. The mother was racked by some kind of lung ailment. The daughter lay-diagnosed it as single pneumonia. Yet due to the family's lack of insurance, coupled with her mother's age, she hadn't brought her to a doctor, figuring there was no point. In the morning she woke up to furious coughing, her mother crying out in pain. Sometimes there were freckles of blood on her pillow and the delicately embroidered handkerchiefs she used to dab her reeking mouth.

When the daughter got home from the Salvation Army, the situation was no worse.

Already in the house's foyer, reeking with mildew and trash from the kitchen, the daughter could hear the mother's retching

echoing down from her bedroom upstairs. It sounded like a choking dog, it sounded like a woman dying. She knew she couldn't face
it yet so she went to the kitchen and poured out a few slugs of Old
Grandad in a juice glass and set it on the kitchen counter, going out
the back door down the stairs in the heat to her little ashcan in the
yard's eastern corner. Even submerged in the shade of the house
the daughter felt sweat trickling down her breastbone, creeping in
rivulets over her ribs. The peafowl that wandered the street behind
hers cried mournfully over the buzzing of insects. Her cigarette was
hot and awful. She didn't know quite what to do with the doll as
she stood in the yard with the cigarette burning and put it near her
in some grass, the plastic bag veiling its face.

Soon enough, she told herself, she'd be able to do this whenever
she wanted. She'd be free of her mother's capacious, slow ruin. She
would own the house outright and then she could sell it. She could
move somewhere else in the world with the profits and live out the
rest of her life unencumbered. And wherever she was she could go
to the bars, but only as long as she wanted to be there and when
she got tired she'd go back to her house, though she more and more
wished it would be an apartment. Even better a condo, sterile as
a church.

She entered the house again still blowing smoke and crossed
the kitchen toward the hallway, shooting down the glass of whiskey.

The same Category 4 hurricane that had knocked the Witch's
Cap askew had partially flooded the front of the house, but the
daughter had never dry-vacuumed it right, opting instead just to
sweep out the water and air-dry the front of the house through
the door. The purple runner carpet, which wound up the stairs,
was irreparably warped and putrid-smelling, and the floor in the
parlor was starting to bow. The daughter found it interesting the

improvements she chose to pay for over others. She'd gone through the last of their limited savings to buy and install a stair-lift on a track so the mother could move comfortably through the house on days the daughter was at work—as much an admission of guilt as affection. The one that she had chosen was considerably expensive: pale grey leather skin with an extra-plush cushion. It was far more, in fact, an admission of guilt.

Now she seated her mother's new doll in the stair-lift. She sent it gliding up the stairs as she tracked alongside it, her eyes on the doll, as though it might get up to mischief. When they got to the landing she watched it a moment sitting slumped in the outsized surround of the chair.

The mother was lying half-tilted in bed, the covers splaying off her body. Her hair was thin and faintly crackling, balding raw across the top. Her cheeks were dry and bony pits. On either side of the headboard were cabinets, glass-fronted and key-locked and crowded with dolls. Victorian dolls with their frilly, dark dresses, Raggedy Ann dolls with vacant, cloth faces, and baby boy dolls in little tuxedos and gowns, their red lips pursed, almost coquettishly. "Evening, mama," said the daughter.

"Mary, Mary, there you are."

The daughter's name wasn't Mary, in fact, but Virginia, though she no longer bothered to correct her mother. Virginia approached her mother's bed, adjusting her against the headboard. She put the doll down in her lap facing up. "A new lovie for you, mama."

It took her a moment to notice the doll, but once she did her eyes stood out with furious, unnatural light. "Oh, Mary, it's precious! It's darling!" she said. She drew the doll up by its arms so that it dangled at her chest.

The doll mooned at Virginia, its eyes laughing at her.

A bitter surge of disappointment came up in the daughter's throat. She had recognized something unspeakably grim that was different than leaving her mother alone without someone to help her all day in the house and different than not taking her to a doctor. She hadn't bought the doll because her mother would love it, she hadn't even bought it to lessen her guilt. No, Virginia had brought the doll home in the end because it repulsed and horrified her and she could see no better way to mock her mother's final torment.

As though on cue, her mother groaned before breaking down into ragged, wet coughing.

The daughter was thin and carrot-haired.

Her long, thin hair fell past her waist. Her face was pale and sharply made, a touch of something feral in it and her figure was trim in a hard, rangy way. Now into her forties it filled her with pride, and she wore the same acid-wash denim cutoffs and scissored-out t-shirts for hair metal bands she had worn as a teen not to make her look younger, she knew that was over, but because it was what she was comfortable wearing. And she always wore flip-flops or sandals of some sort, hating the feel of no air on her toes. Her laugh was sharp, like shattered glass, though her resting expression was one of alertness, an attunement to the fundamental silliness of living that some people mistook for airs.

Sometimes the daughter drank so much Old Grandad the world melted into a grim unreality. That was why she binge-watched her reality shows; the people onscreen were so alien to her, their lives so impossibly far from her own that she started to watch the shows pitying herself, but then by the end she would pity them more in a venomous way that delighted her heart. "Cunt-face salad tosser!" she'd yell at the screen. "Grundle-chafing shit-stick fucker!"

Then, when she'd had her fill, the night would begin to reveal itself to her. She'd find herself in curious places: blinking her eyes in the dark of her yard, drugged by the scent of honeysuckle. She decided she'd meant to end up in these places when she would remember she'd been the next morning but then looking back on the slur of the night she ultimately wasn't sure. Each morning she had pounding headaches. Night-sweats, otherworldly dreams. One morning on the way to work she stopped to throw up in a public trash barrel, wiping her mouth on the hem of her blouse and going in to open up.

The night Virginia bought the doll, she found herself braced in her mother's doorway, her palm sweating around the knob. The lights were blazing in the hall; a wide blade of light hovered over her mother. She stayed there in the door a moment, gazing at her mother's face. Then she pulled the door shut. It was instantly dark. After a while, her eyes could make out a pale mound. She sat by her mother. Took note of her breathing. The frequency of it, how roughly it came. She leaned in closer to her mother, her palm reaching out in the dark of the room to rest against her mother's chest when her fingertips brushed something wrinkly and chilly. Her hand jerked back.

The back of the doll's neck, the flesh-strip across it.

Her mother slept with it, hands clasping its body, the hood pushed back across its shoulders. In her half-drunken state, they appeared almost tender, the small form pressed into the large one, and she thought of herself as she must've been once, in the days before her father died, when the three of them lived happily in the house, though Virginia could scarcely remember it now. Perhaps she'd had a frightening dream. Perhaps she had gone to her mother at midnight, her little whimpers in the dark and her mother held her just like that, her hair fallen across her shoulders.

But no, she remembered, it wasn't like that. Not before her father died and less so after than before. Yes, her mother had always been awful to her, albeit more in secret when her father was alive—a cruel whispered word as they passed in the hall, a home-cooked dinner on her birthday she was guaranteed to hate.

The next day when the daughter woke she sensed her mother's end was near.

A sick pressure clutched at the back of her skull. Her teeth were furred, her mouth bone-dry. She went to the tap and drank glasses of water before making her mother's breakfast.

She always made her mother oatmeal, which was all she could manage to keep down these days. She had started to go up the stairs with the bowl when something nameless called her back. She thought for a moment she needed a drink, just a splash in the juice-glass to level her out, but then she was grappling under the sink for the housecleaning products she never made use of. She lifted out the jug of Drano, placed it on the kitchen counter.

Balancing the oatmeal tray, the daughter ducked sullenly into the room. "Slept well again, Mama?" The mother just hummed. "I made you oatmeal, Mama, here. Let's get you sitting up," she said.

Though these days her mother rarely got out of bed, she never got the sleep she needed. The covers were pushed all the way to the floor. Her mother lay twisted in that week's soiled nightdress. She was moaning with wakefulness, breath sharp and shallow.

Reaching beneath her mother's arms, Virginia pulled her torso close while pushing the bed's pillows back with her palms until they were flush with the carven headboard. It was an intimate and swift maneuver that had necessitated burying her face briefly in her mother's neck as she positioned the pillows. A cathedral of stench stretched above and around her. Virginia changed her diaper, flinching. She excused herself to wash her hands before coming back to the bedside again to make sure her mother was decent in bed, that the hair squeezing out from the sides of her diaper was hidden underneath her gown. Last, she placed the oatmeal on its tray long-ways across her mother's lap but her mother just stared at her, dull and resistant. Virginia knew she was tired of oatmeal for breakfast, just like she was tired of those Heinz mustard sandwiches and lukewarm cottage cheese for lunch, but Virginia had her strategies. "That's oatmeal, Mama. Growing food!"

Her mother had said the same thing to Virginia when she had refused to eat things as a girl. Steamed broccoli? That's growing food! Fatback collard greens? That's growing food! As in, food that was healthy, but made you grow bigger. And she would always choke it down. On past mornings of resistance with her mother and the oatmeal, these words had seemed to trigger something hiding in her mother's mind, the tendons in her spotted arms flexing as she bent her spoon—the irony never once lost on Virginia that her mother was, in point of fact, no longer growing but fading away, yet what else was she going to call it? Existing food? Dying food? But now it made her mother humph.

"Not hungry?" said Virginia in a voice of concern. "Not hungry for your growing food?"

Her mother weakly jerked her head. And Virginia realized though she might've been hungry, quite hungry, in fact, from the evening before when she couldn't recall ever seeing her eat, she didn't want her growing food because it would mean putting down her new doll. "Here," said Virginia and reached for the doll, but her mother's hold on it was shockingly strong.

"No," said her mother. "*No*, I said!"

The gnome doll's legs stretched as the daughter pulled harder. Partly, her mother came up along with it, her arms straining and her torso lifting away from the mountain of pillows, but then she let go and fell back in the bed. "You have to eat, Mama," Virginia explained. "But your lovie can stay with you. See? There we go."

She nestled the gnome doll face first in her arms and began to spoon her mother the oatmeal, that little something extra in it. But even as Virginia did this, alert to how her mother chewed and more alert to how she swallowed, she could feel in some weird, fearful part of herself that something about the doll had changed. The back of its neck appeared transformed—the wrinkly flesh-strip connecting its ears. A tiny space had opened up, interrupting the strip, just above the doll's shoulders. It was as though the flesh-strip was being absorbed by the white porcelain part of it, little by little, and the break in the strip was surprisingly smooth, like a part of the doll just exposed to the air.

Had it always appeared this way? Perhaps the daughter hadn't noticed.

But no, she was sure that the strip had been whole when she'd purchased the doll the day before, continuous across the neck. That didn't stop her either way from spooning the oatmeal until it was gone.

A strange pattern of weeks set in, drifting and soft-focused, there in the house.

Fall breezes stirred up the cinders of summer. Outside, you could comfortably debut a sweater but for Virginia and her mother in the house it was the same.

The daughter would wake up intensely hungover on the thin parlor couch where she often passed out. She'd cure herself with water, whiskey. The mother's breakfast then her own, a chocolate-covered protein bar that earned her the first cigarette of the day. On Halloween, some neighbor brats had hurled eggs and TP, then rocks at the house. One of them smashed through a beveled front window, littering the foyer with wood scraps and glass. Virginia had let the eggs dry in black streaks, the TP disintegrate down through the branches. A storm would clear it all away. But she had never touched the window. The hole in it lessened the trash-mildew stink with fresh, uncanny autumn breezes that blew through the foyer, the parlor, the kitchen, rustling Virginia's hair.

At work, she went into the back of the store where the stockpiles of loose herbs were kept and filched a bit of aconite, popularly known as monkshood. If you steamed it with ginger, it wasn't so deadly. Sometimes downright therapeutic. It had even been used, Virginia knew, to treat respiratory ailments not unlike her mother's. But Virginia didn't want to treat her. In rendering the monkshood, she cut certain corners, ensuring it would still be toxic, just not toxic enough to be instantly fatal, and put the tincture in a jam jar, the jam jar in the highest cabinet. The liquid was a murky brown, something like tobacco spit. Also not unlike brown sugar.

With the tincture, she never exceeded a teaspoonful, and never less than three of sugar. To feed her mother in the morning, she had taken to riding the stair-lift herself with the breakfast tray balanced on her lap, girlishly kicking her legs on ascent, the bannister passing her, muscled and snakelike. Every morning her mother was twisted in bed. She was never without the gnome-doll now. It was her pretty thing, her pet, and her other dolls sat sullenly in their cases like ill-favored children or envious lovers.

Virginia tried not to see that the flesh-strip was changing, the break widening every time she went in. Soon there was almost two inches of space that began to reveal a pristine shade of white, the same shade the face of the doll must've been when whoever first owned it had purchased it new.

A bureau with a wide mirror stood opposite her mother's bed and every time Virginia fed her, she'd watch herself doing it there in the glass: spooning the growing food into the mouth, smoothing back the mother's hair. It grew easy to convince herself she wasn't performing these actions at all, but someone just like her who lived in the mirror, emerged to do the daughter's bidding. There were other times though when she saw not herself but the tight-cornered, chuckling eyes of the gnome. Its wispy beard was growing matted. The tip of its nose showed a greenish black scuffing. Feeding and changing and cleaning her mother, she tried to avoid ever touching the doll. The one time she had, on its little plump belly, the skin and perhaps underneath it was warm. Horrified, she flinched and dropped it. It made a dull thud when it fell on the floor. The doll lay facedown on the carpet, the flesh-strip all but non-existent, the white of the neck like a grotesque return to innocence that never was.

"Poor sweetheart!" her mother said, bullying forward. Virginia had to hold her back. In her moribund state she was jarringly strong.

"Butterfingers," she croaked at Virginia, fell back.

So there was the old bitch again, thought Virginia.

She leaned down to retrieve the doll. She knew that it was not alive. And yet she suspected, absurdly perhaps, that her mother's lifeline was now tied to the doll's, to the pink strip of flesh that stretched over its neck. As though maybe the flesh-strip were only recording the mother's life force as it dwindled in her, like a ledger, or some sympathetic accounting. A lifeline, like one that you'd find on your palm, but here on the back of a thrift store doll's neck—and a lifeline that was always changing the closer and closer it got to its end. She could've upped the monkshood dose. Could've fixed her a bowl brimming full with the stuff. Knowing even as she did that the increase might have no effect on her mother, that only once the strip receded, the back of the doll's neck a uniform white, only then would her mother give up her last breath. The symptoms of the deadly plant were vomiting, fever, and cardiac horrors, but she'd seen none of these in her mother, not yet.

So maybe her mother was already dead. Yes, maybe her mother was already dead, but the daughter was so used to having her there, caring for her each day in the same exact way, she hadn't noticed she'd succeeded.

But no, the mother was alive. The mother needed to be changed, the mother needed to be fed. And still the same question would nag at Virginia: when the flesh-strip receded completely, what then?

When the mother could no longer do for herself, but before her condition had gone to the dogs, Virginia took her grocery shopping.

It wasn't because they lacked quality time. She was sick of her mother as it was. But making the groceries so tuckered her out, it allowed Virginia peace and quiet. All she had to do was suffer through the ordeal of her mother's wheelchair stalling out in the aisles, her inane particularities regarding her diet and after an hour or so they'd be home, the mother snoring in her wheelchair. One time, they were making their way through the store when a woman in church clothes who lived in the town whose face Virginia recognized because it was flabby and slightly sunburned beneath a shell of ice-blond hair got trapped behind her mother's chair and insisted on making small talk with her. For her part, Virginia kept bagging up leeks and throwing them viciously into the basket built onto her mother's chair. This was still in the days when she actually cooked. That night, she intended to make a frittata. "Well, bless you," the flabby-faced woman was saying. "It's not everyone's life that the good lord makes easy."

"You're sweet," said the mother, "but I get by fine."

"Me, I'm just a Christian woman who goes through life with both eyes open…" the flabby-faced woman was babbling on, but Virginia had already blocked out her voice. And she would've continued to block out her voice had she not heard something that made her look up. "…your sister, she's the one that's sweet, taking you out to make groceries like this."

Sudden pain shot through Virginia. It wasn't the pain of vanity but something new, a loneliness, and it plunged through the cave of her, spreading its wings. If she had only had a sister, a brother, a father who lived on this earth, anyone to take her side growing up all alone under scourge of her mother and help her in the years that followed, she wouldn't have been standing here, a tangle-haired and curd-faced drunk, mistaken for someone two decades her senior, jamming root vegetables she could only cook half of in a thin plastic bag she could not seem to open. Virginia held her head up higher. She locked the woman in a stare while snapping out the plastic bag, feeling suddenly capable, powerful even, when her mother's wheelchair powered over her toe. Another, realer pain shot through her.

"Sorry, sister," said her mother.

On the last day of the mother's life the daughter fixed a special breakfast.

Fall had shriveled into winter, the garden a tangle of weeds and stripped branches. The vines had dropped seedpods then withered to jerky. Virginia hadn't paid the light bill and the heat in the house had been shut off for days. She wandered the rooms huddled under a blanket with the cold coming in through the hole in the window, the kind that got into your bones. Today the sun brightened the filth of the kitchen as she sat on the floor against any good sense, cooking on a butane stove.

She could've fixed her mother oatmeal but felt that the woman deserved something better. So Virginia made her sausage, beans, and eggs sunny-side-up with the yolks soft and runny. After putting the eggs on the plate with the rest, she punctured the yolks so the meal slid together. Spooned a quarter-teaspoon of the Aconite mixture and stirred the beans to mask the color.

Her mother's bedroom lay in darkness. She set the breakfast on the sideboard, crossed the room and drew the curtains. Sunlight slashed into the room. It spread across her mother's body, the gnome-doll pressed against her chest.

Virginia went to her bedside to shake her awake, but she'd only been shaking her mother a moment when Virginia realized there was no need to feed her. Her pillow was nearly soaked through with wet blood, chunks of something in the mix. Her eyes were open. Vacant, staring.

A mosquito feasted at her hairline.

To be sure, Virginia put her palm against her mother's mouth and waited. She felt her hand prickling for warmth but none came. To be doubly sure, she got down on her knees, head level with her mother's mattress and put her ear against the lips.

She folded herself into bed with her mother, her head against her mother's chest. And nothing, not even the smell could've stopped her from nuzzling in her mother's neck with her mother's chin pressing down onto her head, like some foolish memory of safety and warmth that, guided by instinct, she'd come there in search of. What she felt was complicated: relieved her mother was at peace and Virginia no longer responsible for her, but also finally sad to lose her, so used to her presence, damaging as it was, now as it had been when Virginia was young, but most of all that loneliness, done spreading its wings and now ruffling to perch. She said her mother's name: "Shereen." And when her mother's eyes stayed closed, she said it again. "Shereen. Shereen. ShereenShereenShereenShereenShere—"

The daughter hadn't heard that name in what now seemed like many years. It was a name her mother hated for as long as she'd been able to remember it was hers—a "lowborn trashy fool girl name" that she'd sought to erase with the name of her daughter. "Virginia's power's in her name," she had once heard her mother explain to her father one night in their room when they thought she was sleeping in the years before her father died. "She'll do something good in a world that hates goodness."

But her mother was wrong, she was part of that world. Goodness seemed to hate her too.

Shifting slightly in the bed, the daughter's elbow brushed the doll. It blazed in the sheets with mammalian warmth, the cloth of its torso stretched tight as a drum. She saw the flesh-strip had returned, traversing completely the back of the neck. But it no longer horrified her. Now it just made her sad, like a hideous child.

She unfolded herself from her mother's embrace and gathered up her mother's meal.

"Mary, Mary, there you are." The daughter paused in the door with the tray in her arms. She mustn't, mustn't turn around. "Mary, Mary, so contrary, where are you going with my food?" Her mother was sitting bolt upright in bed. She held the gnome-doll to her chest and she grinned at the daughter, blood caught in her teeth.

At once, the daughter dropped the tray, the meal exploding at her feet.

Shereen was laughing and then she was coughing, more blood slipping down the front of her gown, and then for the first time in almost five years she was getting up out of her bed by herself, whipping the covers with terrible spryness. Shereen planted her pale, veiny feet on the floor and started to come at the daughter, still laughing. Or it wasn't a laugh, not all the way, but a strange, barking mixture of laughter and coughing, the laughter of a choking dog, the laughter of an undead woman, and as Shereen went by her bureau, her back reflected in the glass, the daughter could see on the back of her neck a strip of flesh that matched the doll's. The strip was puffy, slightly slick. It covered the back of her neck, ear to ear. Though not in the way she had originally intended, he daughter's growing food had worked.

The daughter slowly backed away as Shereen's feet walked over the mess of her breakfast, the plate shards cutting up her feet and the sausage and beans mushing up through her toes, but neither the cuts nor the mess slowed her down. To the contrary, even, Shereen moved faster as the daughter backed faster away down the hall, feeling behind for the place where the hallway ended and the track of the stair-lift began. But she already saw that this wasn't the end. For the daughter, there would never be.

No end to the coughing. No end to the low, childish babble. No end to the oatmeal: four spoonfuls of sugar, and one of the mixture she kept in the cupboards. Again, she'd have to kill her mother until the strip of flesh receded. Or else she'd have to kill the doll. But even if she managed to kill a thing that was not alive, there was no guarantee that her life would be different, that the promise of all she had hoped for herself wouldn't slip, inch by inch, into nothing at all.

THE BACHELOR'S TALE

I. THE INTERVIEW

Concerning the Underwood House and its Makeup- The Narrow Strait- The Gentleman Colleague and All That He Said- Ruminations on a Bachelor's Prospects- The Lady of the Manor- Notes on the Underwood Family and Its Provenance- Sebastian & Cora Underwood- The Chat

What I noticed first about Underwood House was not the thing that drew the eye.

I did not see its scalloped gables, nor the tall lancet windows beneath its pitched attic, nor its Tudor-style porch weathered faintly gray-green, nor even still the clutching trees that halfway hid the entryway through which I, Isaac Lillie, antiquities agent of the Bingham & Haverhill house in Manhattan, would now make my way to deliver a knock. But rather instead the empty moat that surrounded the mansion in perfect circumference, a blackened trench, fifteen feet deep, without a drop of moisture in it.

"Leave me with a card?" I said to the driver dispatched to the station to greet me.

He handed me one from the front without speaking and when I'd alighted he rumbled away.

I stood for a beat at the head of the path leading over the moat to the house's front door while the driver's exhaust dissipated behind me, my bags arranged about my feet. A dog could be heard barking somewhere inside. There were no faces in the windows.

I had not crossed the moat halfway when the heavy oak door to the house shuddered open and a man who was roughly my age careered through it. "You are out of line, Madam! Far, far out of line!" the gentleman said, gesturing with his briefcase. He was speaking to someone beyond the front door but from where I stood I could not make her out. "I leave you an insulted man. Mr. Stoneham *will* hear of your loathe indiscretion." He whirled around amidst his waistcoat and, without looking up, he made fast down the walk.

"I say," I called out, with the man charging at me. A yard away, he stopped and stared. He started out right and I started out right; he started out left and I aped him, absurdly. "I say," I said softer, "if you're in a hurry, I would gladly back up and allow you to pass."

"Someone must," he said, "back up."

"Then let it rest on me, good friend."

And the gentleman nodded in spite of himself.

The door of the house had been open a crack as though Mrs. Underwood, someone, were listening. Then by some unseen force it closed. A complex-sounding series of latches engaged. I started to back toward the head of the path while the man started toward me with only his briefcase. "Mr. Stoneham, you said," as I made my way backward. "Mr. Stoneham of Stoneham and Cross, I presume?"

"Yes that is the one," said the man, his eyes on me and taking me in for perhaps the first time.

"You fellows acquire the most wonderful stuff—Hepplewhites, Sheratons, Chippendales, Phyfes—damn this tricky little path!" I hit a loose patch on the walkway and stumbled. At last I made good ground again and the gentleman came with a couple quick strides. "I'm with Bingham and Haverhill House. Isaac Lillie." I set down my luggage and held out my hand.

But he only stared at it as though it were filthy. The gentleman wandered away through the trees.

"Sir?" I called after him. "Sir, excuse me? Would you like me to call you a car back to Brocton?"

Dusting my pants in vexation, I watched him. Now the world was still again.

Re-crossing the moat was a trickier business, but I thought of Cordelia to steady my steps and I thought of her, really, the last time I'd seen her, on the day I had asked her would she be my wife, at which her face had darkened slightly with something uncertain and sad, a withholding. But then the gloom had gone from her and she had given her reply.

"Of course," a woman's voice spoke up, "he did not have your pure blue eyes." I'd been so absorbed in re-crossing the moat I had not heard the front door unlatching again and had not seen the female presence now filling the sizable doorway before me.

"Splendid morning," I said. "You must be Lady Cora?"

She politely demurred. "Mrs. Underwood, please."

I could not cover my surprise. She was a glossy, blood-full thing no more than five and twenty years—or anyway did she appear—and her dress was Victorian, too, an antique, with its piping and ruching and Mameluke sleeves. Her dark hair was taken down a la Madonna, her face sharp-boned, unmarked and white. "You must excuse the Stoneham boy. He was of the excitable species," she said.

I had the urge to clear my throat, but told my hostess, "Not at all."

Unable quite to meet her eyes, I broke my eyes upon the gloom of what I assumed was the house's foyer in hopes of maybe seeing there any one of the century pieces I'd come for but saw instead two sets of feet, one in Oxfords, one in slippers, precisely aligned at the edge of the dark. "Sebastian, my eldest and Cora, my daughter," she said of the two person-shapes that emerged.

The right one was a thin young man with eyes and hair as dark as hers, the left his twin in all save this: while the young man's sharp features and dark prominences imbued him with something half-wild and conspiring, the girl, who was likely no more than eighteen, had made plentiful good on the seed of her mother. I at once understood why the men talked about her. Not pretty, not quite, like Cordelia was pretty—my chicken! my heart! now at large in the city, oh how I missed her auburn wafts, her small quick hands, her crooked teeth—but enigmatic, unafraid, and it seemed unaware of her limbs and their languor. She was tall and slim-hipped, with a hillock of bust beneath a white gown less complex than her mother's. And then a little ragged dog—the one, I assumed, I'd heard barking outside—crossed sharply in front of the Underwood woman and continued to bark with a terrible purpose, its tiny teeth flashing, its tongue dabbing pink. It was some advanced genus of Jack Russell terrier.

"Ethelred," the lady said. "Forbear to terrify our guest."

"Ethel," the one named Sebastian called out. "You heel, Ethelred or I'll stitch up that yap!"

And then, so soft I was unsure as to whether or not I had heard her correctly, the girl named Cora said, "You're here."

Mrs. Underwood leading, her children behind, we traveled through the high, dark house.

Ethelred followed behind us not barking, his prune of a nose nearly brushing the floor. No one had taken the bags that I carried—solicitor's papers and some suits of clothes—and the sides of them bumped as we journeyed along. The walls were very close indeed and outfitted with gaslight flues, which led me to reflect en route that my hosts were not nearly as antediluvian as the ranting bad sport in the drive seemed to think. How indignant he'd been about nothing so much as a shower of dust and a little old dog.

There was a smell upon the air. I could only describe it as citrusy, maybe—a sickly sweet astringency—and the boards underfoot had a sodden aspect. They felt mildewed without the stink. A couple rugs were damp as well and gave gentlest suck on the soles of my shoes. They had bad winter storms in this part of the state. I wondered had Underwood House taken water—but my thoughts fled from me at a sonorous tolling, suddenly, right by my ear, which came from the guts of a grandfather clock set back in the hall we were journeying down. "Brash old fellow," I remarked.

The parlor was our destination. We all took up seats that "the chat" might commence. Mr. Bingham had called it that always: "the chat." Which was to say an interview to determine if I was the proper aspirant to auction off gems from the family's estate. Only one agency every year had the privilege and Bingham & Haverhill house had sent me. "Stoneham & Cross, Livermore & Culpepper, those braggarts all have had their day. But never in all these years, dear boy," Mr. Bingham had told me while spinning his pen, "has

Bingham & Haverhill house sent a man that the Underwoods liked well enough to entrust."

"Is that normal?" I'd asked him, upon hearing this.

"Normal," he had said. "Define."

"To interview the auctioneer."

"The hoard that they have at that house out in Brocton is anything *but* normal, boy."

He was also my soon-to-be father-in-law, I see that I might've neglected to mention, and it had been under his influence, surely, that Cordelia's appearance had darkened so sadly on the day, two weeks prior, I'd asked her to marry. Indeed I had had the disturbing impression that he'd sent me to Brocton for solely this reason and that if I failed to return to New York with notaried papers confirming me chosen, my darling's face would darken more. And then she would be lost to me.

"Why not let us start at the start, Mr. Lillie," Mrs. Underwood said. "Tell us: where were you born?"

They all sat down across from me on a Sheraton sofa with delicate reeding—a piece, I thought, which might be mine if I indulged my instincts right—the twins of the house either side of their mother, Sebastian left and Cora right. Ethelred curled in his mistress' lap, a little furry pile of rot. "Baltimore," I answered her.

"And moved to New York City, when?"

"I did not go from there to there. I apprenticed a while with a firm in New Haven."

"Pray tell which one?"

"Batchelder & Smitty."

"I have not heard their name," she said.

"They were an up-and-coming house but they have lately closed their doors."

Mrs. Underwood looked at me level a moment. "Your father," she said, "was he, too, in antiques?"

"My father worked the railroads, Ma'am."

"A conductor?"

"A porter," I said, "I'm afraid. Baltimore, Richmond and then back again."

"They call them corridors, don't they? Crawfish alley, Mr. Lillie."

And here Sebastian laughed a burst, leaning over his mother to touch Cora's knee. "Hear that, sister? Railroad man! I'll bet he lays a heavy tie."

"You're silly, Sebastian," continued his mother in a not altogether sincere tone of voice. "Their father, my husband—*late* husband, of course, as your senior partners have doubtless informed you—was instrumental all his life in designing what travelers now know as the sleeper. Were sleepers on your father's route?"

"There was not time enough to sleep the route my father worked," I said.

"We owe our fortune to the things, your partners have doubtless informed you as well."

Uncomfortable and caught off guard that she had broached financial matters I said to her only, "Condolences, ma'am. It can't be easy, him not here."

"Is there—somewhere—a Mrs. Lillie?"

"Not quite." I backtracked, then amended, "Not yet."

"You are on hiatus?" she said.

"Affianced."

"Ah," said the woman. "A lover in limbo. Sweeten our ears with her name, won't you, dear?"

"Cordelia Bingham," I pronounced.

At these two words, the twins went stiff. As though to console them, their mother said, "Well," and took up each one of their hands in her own. "That does sounds like a sticky business. Jewel in Mr. Bingham's crown. I do hope, Isaac, for your sake, she isn't in a way?" she said.

It was my turn to stiffen then. "No," I said mechanically.

"You are," said Mrs. Underwood, "unpracticed in the ways of flesh?"

"I am—" I coughed "—a gentleman in every meaning of the word."

"A gentleman is not a monk. Or anyway, he need not be."

"I am *no* monk," I might've barked. "Still, my virtue is my pride."

A world-weary mischief came over her face. "And so you love yourself instead."

Of course I could not answer that.

Sebastian was staring at me open-mouthed, in a strange, crumpled posture, arm propped on the couch.

"And do you eat red meat?"

"When served."

"And drink?"

"Just wine."

"And smoke? Foul habit."

"I take a cigar after supper sometimes."

"Moderation makes exception. And how much, on average, do you sleep a night?"

"No less than six hours, ma'am, and no more than nine."

"You bathe regularly?"

"I try."

"And are healthy?"

"As healthy as most men my age."

"You take aerobic exercise?"

"A constitutional, at dusk."

"You stroll?"

"And swim. When I have leisure."

"Not in the Hudson."

"A men's club—uptown."

"Do you ponder, on Sundays, the life of the soul?"

"I am…"

"You're not a Roman, are you?"

"A Methodist, if you must know. Somewhat of a lapsed one, but Kingdomtide-leaning."

"Partake of sweets?"

"Oh figs and dates," I told her with an off-hand air for the answers were starting to slip from my mouth and I had the impression of Underwood's rising to meet my correctness like overripe orchids, the whole unnatural brood of them with their glossy dark hair and their velvety eyes and the heightened interest that came off them in waves, as though they were assessing me like I was assessing the sofa behind them.

But nonetheless I answered on. And soon the interview concluded.

II. AFTERNOON AND EVENTIDE

The Eager Companion- The Midas Room- Taking Stock- Dear Cordelia- The Toll of the Clock- An Afternoon Nap- The Ichor and the Groaning Sound- An Unexpected Visitor- The Dinner Bell

"Is it true," said Sebastian on our way up the stairs to the bedroom where I would be spending the evening, "that Manhattan ladies are so beautiful they seem to float above the pavements?" Again he let fly with that shrill, bubbling laugh. "There are no women like that here—except for my mother and Cora, of course. Well here is your bedroom." He gestured around. "The Midas Room, my mother calls it. I expect, looking round, you will understand why."

Sebastian stepped in and I paused at the threshold. It was all of it, seemingly, there in that room—the Underwood dragon's hoard, hundreds of thousands. A Phyfe dining table wept trembling long light from a Tiffany glass chandelier, right above it, while exceeding a dozen of Hepplewhite chairs were ranged around it boardroom-style. Plus, a Chippendale bed-frame, three Sheraton couches, a Louis XIV escritoire. "It's marvelous. It's simply—well. Whoever imagined…"

"There could be so many?" Sebastian spoke up with an edge to his voice. "Eye-popping impressive collection indeed." But then he appeared to fall into depression; his thin shoulders fell and his eyes combed the floor. "I will leave you to do your ablutions," he said. "I expect we shall dine at some point in the evening."

Just like Mr. Stoneham, he wandered away.

I admit that at first I was taken aback at how abruptly he had gone and I stood staring after his coattails a moment while the Midas Room's centuries settled around me. With a chuckle I cuffed his invisible arm—oh Sebby, you scoundrel! you queer little lamb!—and setting down my bags at last I made a survey of the room. Which seemed to me less of a guest room, in fact, than a master bedroom for the former repurposed. Perhaps the lord and lady's room in the grip of a boundlessly happier age and my heart bucked with sadness to think of Lady Underwood never quite being able to sleep in it now. But I mustn't let sentiment weigh on me so!

There was appraisal to be made.

After touring the room writing down in my daybook the makes and conditions of relevant items, a glad little star penciled next to the prime, I sat before the escritoire to pencil a buzzing succession of letters: the first to my senior colleagues in Manhattan, Mr. Bingham pointedly, to the gist of my having succeeded out here and for them to expect, any day, my return. And the second of course to my sweet bride-to-be in her father's brownstone at the edge of the park who was, at this moment, absorbed in bride's errands or taking an afternoon tea with her mother or, did I even dare to hope, composing a letter, likeminded, to me. She wrote with her right hand just shading her temple while moving her left one down the page, now and then pausing to look at her palm to be sure that she hadn't smeared.

I wrote to her now how completely I missed her, and how beautiful was the passageway north, and how warmly the family had welcomed me there, and how worthwhile was their collection, and how in this capacity her fiancé could scarcely fail.

Just before I signed my name, the clock downstairs intoned at three. After came a muffled rush as of water, perhaps, on its way through the walls. I hitched my pen a moment, listening. Though the whole house might well be outfitted for gas, plumbing was another matter. I poked around beneath my bed and dragged to light a silver pan; in the washroom, an iron tub hunkered for heating. I returned to the desktop and signed off my name but by that time the sound was dwindling, a whistling susurrus that weighted my eyes. I sealed up my letters, and put down my pen, and lay on the bed for a rest.

Then woke up. Something was profoundly wrong.

The big room was baking—or rather I was, although I'd slept above the covers. They must've had the furnace going a few shovelfuls in excess of the season, these drafty houses, after all, and I pulled myself into a sitting position only to find myself bound at the waist. And I saw that indeed I *was* under the covers, the counterpane cutting my abdomen crosswise. It was almost as though I'd been tucked into bed by someone other than myself and I kicked at the ends of my shroud in disgust until I was able to draw up my knees. Extricating myself I swung over the bed and I rested my feet, still in shoes, on the floor. And more perturbing still I saw that I had not removed my coat and the shirt I had planned to repurpose for dinner was utterly soaked through with sweat. A panicked embarrassment rushed to my head that I had missed the supper hour and that my hosts, who'd dined without me, had been too polite to disturb me at rest. Though I calmed when I saw that the room's indistinctness was due to the fact it was only just dusk.

I sneezed hard and fast a succession of times. There was blood with the snot in the crease of my palm.

I hunted blindly through my things to find a dinner-worthy shirt and when I had found it I used the soaked-through one to wipe off my torso before buttoning up. This proved a hasty strategy when small spots of moisture bloomed through the clean fabric, but I went on assembling the buttons regardless, keeping my eyes on the Midas Room's walls.

They struck my mind as, well, tumescent, bending darkly at the seam. There was also some manner of dampness about them, as though they were made of the most porous stone. And it wasn't confined to that part of the wall but seemed to cover all the others—a waterfall of sticky mist that seemed to flow down from some point in the ceiling.

My shirt half unbuttoned, my brow pouring sweat, I walked to the wall that my bed stood against and watched the moisture on the flock. I lighted a candle set next to my bed. I put a finger to the stream and found it not a stream at all but rather a grease or a film—say, an ichor, the same sort of citrusy stench coming off it. And what was more the wall itself was strangely buoyant to the touch, and though I was loathe to acknowledge it, fleshy. And as my cheek grew closer still the better to hear it and see was it breathing, a commoner aspect pervaded my nose: the blackened smell of paper burning. "Damn!" I said. Then, "Double damn!"

The candle was singeing the wallpaper blackly. I yanked back the flame just before it took up. The wall seemed to shudder, a sick, heaving motion, as though it were flinching, as though I had *burned it*. A knock came at the bedroom door.

"Please God not now," I said aloud as I rubbed at the wall with the tail of my shirt.

Cora stood inside the door. She toed the threshold, dark head lowered. She was wearing an evening dress, pearl gray with ruffles, and underneath her chest was heaving, as though she could not catch her breath—as though my presence made her anxious. She saw me see her, did not flinch but continued stare at me, hungry, impassive.

"Have you come here to fetch me for dinner?" I asked but before I could ask her to sit she was gone. I crossed the room to, maybe, catch her, I am not really sure what I wanted to do and when I arrived at the mouth of the hall my candle cut instantly down through the dark and showed Cora Underwood there at the end, looking back over her shoulder at me.

III. THE DINNER

Adrift in the Darkness- The Dining Room Table- Peculiarities of
the Underwood Diet- Concerning Mr. Langford- The Tyrants of
City Living- Theophilus Underwood- A Standard Made Good
On

Ten minutes later, made hastily over, I picked my way downstairs
for supper, assuming that Cora's bizarre overture had been a sort
of call to table. But as I said the house was dark and few of the gas
flues outfitted with lanterns, just a couple of sconces at long intervals along the halls and down the stairs, and I got turned around
several times as I searched, coming first to the parlor and then the
library before fetching up in the bright dining room where the
Underwood family was already seated. I'd rounded a corner and
there it was, floating, oasis of light in the ancestral dark.

Across from Mrs. Underwood an empty place was set for me.
"Cora says you've had a doze. You must be starving, Mr. Lillie."

I went to the sideboard where four plates were stacked and
taking one went down the line while the Underwoods watched
from their Hepplewhite table. I heard too distinctly the sloughing
of meat and the spooning of beets and the slopping of lentils as
I made my plate beneath their eyes, and though I'd felt uncomfortable the sight and the smell of the food made me wild.

I sat with my food and unfolded my napkin while the
Underwood family arose one by one, the next one only standing
up when the person assembling her plate had sat down. When Mrs.
Underwood was served, we all began to eat at once—I ravenously,
surprising myself, while out of the corners of my eyes the hands

of the Underwoods lifted and fell with what then seemed alarming slowness, and Ethelred the mangy toy went weaving in among our legs. Watching me eat, Mrs. Underwood said, "We offered you nothing substantial at lunch."

"Think nothing of it," I said. "Just delicious." Or truthfully said in between charging mouthfuls, never mind that the chicken had been overcooked and that the lentils were unseasoned.

"What is your assessment, then?" Mrs. Underwood asked of the top of my head.

"The pieces in my room?" I said. She nodded her head. "They are specimens, Madam."

"There are more in the buildings out back."

"Aren't there?"

The matriarch studied me chewing a moment. "We have furnished this house in accord with the hope we should never have reason to leave it. The city tends to come to us. And yet," her lip twitched, "you are different from them, these ambitious young cads who flock in from the bowery."

"We are cut, as they say, from the same grasping cloth."

"Well we chose *you*."

"You did," I said. "I am sure very soon you will come to regret it."

"It pleases you?" Sebastian said. He was leaning far back and far down in his chair.

"I must admit it does," I said. "I had wanted, of course…" And my throat became dry. "I had wanted, of course, to be chosen by you. And yet I suppose what you're hitting upon when you say, Mrs. Underwood, ma'am, I am different, is that compared to some, I am. I have never been one to expect anything."

"There was a man much like yourself. Langford was his name," she said. "He, too, was from the city south. A company man seeking signature pieces to buy and resell, as they do every year. But this man was different. Like you, I suppose, though different on another spectrum. He ravaged *Cora* in her bed." She savagely whispered the name of her daughter. "Cora didn't understand for I hadn't yet spoken to her of such things. He took her, my daughter, and made her his minion. And all I could do was insist that he leave. And so when I talk of corruption," she snarled, "you too will know the thing I mean." As she spoke I had shifted my gaze to Sebastian, who I had seen move from the edge of my eye and sat with his plate on the flat of his knee where Ethelred was getting at it. "A man dithers into the port in the morning," Mrs. Underwood said, making legs with her hands, "and by six in the evening he's losing at Monte, a slattern girl upon his arm. But you are not that sort, are you, Mr. Lillie of Bingham & Haverhill House?"

My expression was rigid; my face birthed a smile. My mortification was streaming from me. I let my eyes alight on Cora, whose misfortune and shame was the source of our chat, but she was too busy not eating her food.

"Theophilus possessed such a conscience," she said. "Theophilus *there*, you see." And pointed just above my head, to the paneled wall-space that surmounted the mantle. It was immense, the figure study, and it was absurd that I'd not seen it there. Or maybe I'd seen it but chose to ignore it, not wanting to broach the unthinkable subject: a man in a midnight blue suit with blond whiskers, on his lips an expression of bored irritation.

"He looks terribly young to have died. I am sorry." I retired my utensils. "I hope it was peaceful."

"The opposite I fear," she said. "He drowned in the moat that encircles the house. It used to have water inside it—much water. One winter he slipped from the edge and he drowned. The freezing had him, I would bet, before the water filled his lungs. And so we had it drained," she said. "That is how we live today."

Taken aback at her bleak candidness, I paused for a moment and studied my plate. "My heart cries out to hear your loss."

"I can tell that it does by your face," said the lady, placing a hand at the top of her breast. "You are so apparently real, Mr. Lillie. Almost too good to be true, one suspects. Theophilus had standards." She nodded at me. "I am guessing you would've fulfilled most of them."

IV. ABED

The Nightmare- The Unsavory Business- Pursuit and Discovery- The Unshod Flues and What They Meant- A Troubled Respite- The Search for What He Could Not Say- Turn-of-the-Century Gentleman's Fashion- Suppositions on the Prospects of His Untold Predecessors

The dream was of my wedding night.

Or so I was able, somehow, to determine and found me suspended facedown, my limbs mobile, inside a brightly lighted space. I knew it was my wedding night not only because the dream logic conferred it but also because of the following things realized in succession by me in the dream. First: the space I hung amidst could be no other place than the Bingham house parlor, with Mr. Bingham's ashtray there, the hollowed-out hoof of a deer, embers in it. Second: I saw all around me, in piecemeal, the faces of Cordelia's parents and the faces of mine and of relatives sundry, forming a sort of horseshoe gallery. Third: Cordelia was beneath me, lying upright on some manner of palette whereas I hung above her as though by a harness—and covering her loveliness, the part of her south of her pretty, bare shoulders, a layered integument of blankets and quilts with a scandalous hole burrowed just past the waist. And I was being lowered down, the harness creaking as I went while faces spoke up from the guest-gallery and Cordelia appeared to rise up underneath me. "Steady as she goes it, dear," said my mother from somewhere outside of the light. "There's an Izzie. There's a boy."

And I woke up to Cora, her mouth closed around me.

Her eyes, below my waist, flashed up. I could not see myself down there and I thought for a moment I'd been mutilated but then I saw that Cora's mouth was completely around me, lips pressed to my pelvis and that the infinity felt in the dream had been the dark of Cora's throat. I was, I could feel, on the verge of completion.

I jackknifed my body and pushed Cora from me. "No more of this—no!" I commanded absurdly. And as her lips detached from me in a long trembling skein of saliva, she grunted. In her night-dress she scrambled backward off the bed, fetching up at the edge where she wiped at her mouth. And then, staring at me for several more seconds with her face half obscured by the cave of her hair, she rose on her haunches like some kind of jackal and loped from the room practically on all fours.

I sat in the darkness, outrageously tumid.

The bedroom around me was baking again and the walls once again had that sticky mist on them. I groaned and I ripped off the sweat-dampened covers and I ran to the still open door in my nightdress, and peering down the dim hallway where the same ineffectual sconces were burning I looked for Cora at the end but saw just the dark of the wall at the branching. I moved partway into the hall and, sensing something off, looked down.

I darted back into the bedroom again and I counted to thirty, my eyes squinted shut.

The house beyond the room was warm, yet with pockets of cold that swirled over my ankles. The same rushing sound I had heard hours before when I'd written my letters moved again in the walls.

I rounded the bend on yet more darkened hallway and, down at the branching, a dim figure, standing. It was facing the woodwork, its back facing me. I could not make out who it was and I went toward it slowly, my eyes straining forward, my bare feet freezing on the stone. "Cora," I called to the wall-facing shape. "A misunderstanding between us, all right?"

Yet still the figure did not turn.

I am ruined, I thought to myself, I am dirtied. I am chasing a sinister girl through the gloom and halfway down the passage paused with half a mind to turn around. The candles threw terrible shapes on the flock and the flock undulated, secreting its ichor, and the figure grew closer to me through the gloom in the same way Cordelia had done in the dream. It stood with its hands hanging down at its sides, its neck arched up and faintly straining. It did not wear a nightdress on it but rather a scarlet and dark green affair, and by and by I realized whose closed-off form I stood before. "Mrs. Underwood? Madam?" I said reaching out to touch the figure on its shoulder.

But scarcely had I said these words than I perceived another sound—a sort of slurp amid the groaning. Mrs. Underwood turned. I stepped back a few paces.

There was something resplendently wrong with her face.

Difficult to see at first in the shivering shadows that fell from the sconces but then I saw her eyes were black, like onyx marbles in her skull and that her skin had gone translucent, like rice paper, say, or the skin of a corpse and that under the skin her anatomy streamed with befouled tributaries of living, black blood. The slurp I had heard was her sipping the flue—sipping something *out* of it—further evidenced now in the tarry, black stream that ran down from her mouth. "Mr. *Lillie*," she said, genuinely surprised. "Why you should be in bed, asleep."

The unshod flue behind her head was trickling with the same black fluid and I backed further from her, palms raised at my chest. I said, "I was… I thought… I just…"

"You just would what, my dear?" she said.

No end to my buffoonery as I turned on my heels and began to run from her. And heading down the next hallway, at the section of wall just across from my bedroom, someone else was standing there—most likely Sebastian, I knew by his tails—who seemed to be drawing the same sustenance that his mother had drawn from the flue in the wall. He turned toward me casually, dipping his head.

And his a cursed heredity, with his eyes and his veins in the candle-flame, blackly, with the same drool of black from the sides of his mouth. I ran past Sebastian and into the bedroom where I shielded myself in the lee of the door. "We will laugh about this over breakfast!" I called.

I managed now to slam the door.

And did the thing I might've done: I leaned on the wood and slid down on my back. The terrier slammed on the door from outside, a hardier blow than I might've imagined and when the barrier held strong began to rake it with her claws. The first thing that occurred to me was how I might still save the deal; whether my having seen in the night what I'd seen was grounds for severance of my interests—for though the Underwoods were queer, was their queerness in fact such a consummate threat?

But this too brought a wave of shame. Had I so little self-respect?

I remembered what Cora had just then done to me—her vacant, dark eyes flashing up from my waist. I sat at the base of the door in a shambles, my face cradled into my hands and I heaved. I did not weep, though felt I might. My flesh was mortified and sick. I felt wretched, humiliated, but also guilty and uncouth, as though I had done unforgivable wrong. And then in its wake a pervasive, cold numbness.

I think that I sat there for longer than planned on.

Not composed in the least, I changed out of my nightshirt and put on the trousers and whites of that day, and I started to hunt through the densely packed room for what telltale I could not say. I was looking for something, a riddle, a notion that had till that moment evaded my mind and I tore through the stained, empty drawers of the desk and I dragged my arms underneath tables and couches and I ripped off the bedclothes, inverted my pockets, perused the walls for secret panels.

The card of the driver who'd brought me from Brocton floated down to the boards at my feet. I retrieved it. Hideously it was blank of all words and I let it fall back to the floor.

I ran to the one place I hadn't yet looked, the closet where I'd hung my clothes and turning out each of my suits in succession—I'd packed three good ones just in case—I flung them, hissing, down the rack where they gathered in rumpled, dark shapes in the corner. There was something back there past the first row of hangers, a second dimension of closeted space. My hand brushed objects, soft and grainy. Holding my candle aloft, I pressed in.

Rows upon rows of men's suits hung inside it, twenty on the outside margin. Mr. Underwood's suits? I began to file through them. And then with sharp nausea began to perceive that each was of another age, the lapels growing wider, the tails lengthening, the pleats becoming more defined, as though the advancement of gentleman's fashion were slowly decaying in front of my face and what was more, I realized, the suits were all of different sizes, this one for a man twice as tall as I was, this one for a man who was shorter but broader.

Which one of them belonged to Langford? was the first thing that vacantly came to my mind. Which one of them had touched his skin, the last protection he had worn?

I staggered away and my foot rattled something.

In a bucket, a forest of gentlemen's canes.

V. COFFEE

The Solicitor Rallies- Pleasantries- A Sudden Deterioration of Circumstance- The Command Performance- Adjournment for the Afternoon- The Men on the Lawn and the Objects They Carried- Though He Would Rather Not, A Doze

Predictably, I had not slept and I stayed in my bedroom till well after nine.

The autumn sun came through the clouds and paled the room along its edges. The hardier of birds still chirped. Ethelred was barking somewhere, high and frenzied, deep within. I crept downstairs without my bag, having packed and then stowed it the evening before.

And yet, you see, I had not fled.

I hope for this fact that I may be forgiven. For in spite of the many un-savvy young sorts in penny dreadfuls you have read who choose *not* to flee when the threat is so plain, remanding themselves to a terrible fate that with recourse to foresight they might have avoided, I remembered that I, Isaac Lillie, was real and not a man inside a book. Indeed I was a man in full with a name to uphold, a woman to wed and professional connections of importance to maintain, and I would not turn tail and run from a midnight encounter with rural eccentrics.

I was, at that, a gentleman. I would see my sojourn through its final upset.

And there was still all that besides I'd told the Binghams in my letter—my commitment to them vis-à-vis the assignment—the upheaval of which, at this stage in the game, might bring about in them a total reversal. This stamped correspondence I carried with me inside the pocket of my coat.

As I wended a path toward the Underwood's parlor, the way ahead seemed not at all the astral plane it had last night but merely an old country house down at heel, diffuse autumn sun lying down on the boards. How lovely it was to be warm and inside, indubitable among all human comforts! The sound of the makings of coffee and cake from the parlor ahead of me buoyed this feeling. And although there was also that citrusy smell that never really went away, introducing a queer underlay to the coffee and the smell of baked sugar that swirled at the branching, I must admit that I was pleased to enter the room on the Underwood family, so handsome and vital and all of a piece on the Sheraton couch where I'd been interviewed what was now, it came to me, a full day before.

I sat with my hands folded over my knees before the breakfast they had laid.

"Good morning, Mr. Lillie, sir," said the Underwood matriarch, pouring me coffee. "We are all of us getting a jump on the day."

"Madam, Lady, Lord," I said to the seated tableau of my hosts in that order and each of them smiled at me, perfectly mellow—each of them except for Cora, whose face was obscured by a fan of dark hair that wafted and shimmered with strenuous combing—and everything seemed as it ought to have seemed as I sipped at my coffee and broke off my cake. The sun crested cover and streamed through the pane. "I trust you all slept well," I said.

Mrs. Underwood smirked. "Pass the crumble, Sebastian."

Looking at me, he said, "There, mother dear."

Mrs. Underwood prodded her plate without eating. "I shouldn't ask the same of you."

"Nonsense, Mrs. Underwood. I slept like the Kraken, in spite of the heat."

"The heat," Sebastian said. "Of course."

"You must have a powerful furnace downstairs."

Mrs. Underwood sighed at that. "Old drafty houses."

"Pass the butter, mother, please."

"Not before you pass the cream."

And so they continued to pass back and forth over sullen, coiffed Cora the trappings of breakfast, letting components accrue on their plates without ever actually taking a bite—the muffins, the berries, the sugar, the jam while Cora sat there, china barren, with her dress buttoned high and her hair in her face.

"In fact I slept so well," I said, "in that cozy old overstuffed room where you put me that when I woke I could have sworn I was back in my quarters on Battery Park."

My face was clenching rigidly; I suppose you might call it a smile in some circles. I belted my coffee back, scalding my mouth.

And then, like a painting set fire from behind, the scene before me seemed to char, spots of ruin eating through in places that I might've missed: the tarry abyss of the coffee I held; Sebastian's wet teeth in his half-open mouth; the citrusy smell, which now struck me as cloying, like orchids in a dead man's room; Cora Underwood's shimmering, worked-over hair that fell to the side for a moment, no more, and I saw that the skin underneath had been blackened below the eye and on the cheek as though someone had walloped her face open-handed.

Everything was not all right. Yet here I was, still sitting here.

"*She* was drawn to *you*, of course. One suffering creature in heat to another. But I am explaining to you, Mr. Lillie?" Mrs. Underwood told me while swirling her coffee.

Cora Underwood's hair fell back over her face. "Freshen your coffee?" Sebastian inquired.

Without my assent he got up from the couch and he lowered his long, wolfish limbs over me with the spout of the pot leading down from his arm. I watched the dark stream of it plash in my cup, and remembered the gas flue's unholy excretions, and when I looked up there was fear in my face. Hand shaking a little, I sipped from my cup.

Mrs. Underwood looked at me level and smiled. "If you'll only remain with us here through the day while we yoke and outfit you a city-bound wagon, then every item you desire will be your firm's on good consignment."

"Must it be through the day?"

"You are hurrying off?"

"I am scheduled for lunch…"

"Somewhere else?"

"…at the Bingham's."

"I should think that your putative father-in-law would understand why you are late. Your tenure continues as needed," she said.

I supposed that I still had the job after all.

The sun dipped back behind the clouds and the family repaired to their rooms after breakfast, I assumed to wash up for a tour of the grounds or a trip to the stables I'd seen from my window, yet having heard nothing by way of a plan and feeling a little bit wary, besides, I remained, just the heirlooms and me, in my room, hoping to comfortably wait out the day. My bag was packed, my letters sealed. I had made my selections of note for the firm.

All that remained between me and Manhattan, between me and Cordelia, was one ready wagon.

I cogitated on this plan while staring out the western window, which held a view of trodden lawn occasioned with a couple pines, beyond the pines a stable-house and beyond that just shadowed woods that might go on for many miles. The Underwoods seemed all alone.

Yet not wholly alone, I saw. There were two figures bearing an angular bulk from the doors of the stable and over the lawn where they set it to rest in the bed of a wagon. I could only assume that the item they carried was the Sheraton couch I'd proposed taking with me, the very same one where I'd sat for the "chat," the figures who bore it the Underwoods' men, though they were the only domestics I'd seen. Indeed, there had been all throughout my deployment a curious absence of house staff at all, and the tableau of them moving goods to the bed across the pale grass in the afternoon light was one that had seemed to appear before me without intimation of previous movement, as though someone had stamped it there upon the parchment of the pane. What looked like the Sheraton sofa was followed by what also looked like the Phyfe dining table and this followed, too, by the Hepplewhite chairs. And yet, when at some point I turned from the glass to make a survey of the room, recognizing that most of the items in transit had been inside it just this morning, I saw that it remained unchanged. Every item was still in its previous place.

I set up a chair looking out on the lawn where I could watch the happenings and I watched the scene dully though not without hope: it was just what my hostess had told me would happen—me here in my room while the wagon was loaded. And so while the furnace heat raged in my room, and the clock tolled in the hall downstairs, and that sinuous rushing sound moved in the walls, I stared at the featureless, dark shapes of men moving featureless, dark shapes of things to the wagon when before very long, though I rallied not to, I felt myself drop off to sleep.

VI. UNDERWOOD

Half-Glimpsed Revelations- The Hallway, Again- Cora Underwood Stands at the Foot of the Stairs- Circumlocutions- A Proposal Laid Bare- From the Depths of the Moat- Decisions, Decisions- The Last Redoubt- Gentleman's Etiquette Put Into Practice- The Fate of the Letters

For the third time I woke up in Underwood House.

I was still sitting there in my chair at the window, yet a couple

feet lower than when I'd dozed off, slithering down in the chair as I slept until I sat twisted half off of my seat. The house must have some soporific effect, I thought in a dim paranoia, awaking. The house is subduing me, making me soft. The house is marinating me. But these gruesome figments I pushed from my mind. The windowpane was fogged and dim.

I rubbed away the moisture there and saw by the sky it was getting on twilight. And just for a moment the same panic gripped me that I was late again for supper until I remembered today was today, the very same day I was scheduled to leave and forever be quit of the Underwood House.

The men on the lawn were still loading the wagon, stacking this item congruent to that. Or maybe they were loading off, perhaps to stand back and assign better placement, for the same shrouded objects I'd seen being borne from the stable-house doors to the bed of the wagon were now being borne back again to the doors and grouped on the lawn in a haphazard congress. They moved against the pink dusk-light like automata on a spindle and once the last item was set in grass, without even pausing, they carried them back.

Terror, like a bottle fly, was buzzing back behind my eyes.

I straightened my necktie. I gathered my things. The clothes I wore were sweated through—inundated with sleep-sweat my every possession—but I did not have time to change before opening my door on the unlighted hall.

The way ahead was dim and still. The house seemed to bask in the stillness of twilight. The only sounds that reached my ears were the pad of my shoes on the arabesque rugs, the creak of my leather suitcase swinging from me, and my breath raking dry in my throat from the heat as the hall tunneled onto an airy rotunda that overlooked the entryway.

The stillness here was more intense, though the foyer was pink from the sunset outside. It was as though I stood inside a mansion-sized blossom of quartz.

I took the master staircase slowly, watching it unwind beneath me and when I had got, say, a third of the way I saw a figure down below. Cora Underwood stood on the bottommost step in the grey evening dress that exposed her pale shoulders. Even halfway down the stairs I could still see the bruise underneath her left eye.

At first she did not move or speak. Then she reached around behind her back and started to fumble at something complex which as soon as her décolletage fell away I realized were her dress' stays. She peeled the dress away from her, and she was naked underneath, and she stepped gingerly from the fall of the skirt, and she stood white and pink in the puddle of fabric, watching me with a sort of benumbed melancholy. The light outside was reddening. Cora Underwood looked like an icon of blood. And the grandfather clock it was tolling again, and the rushing was rampant again in the walls, and recalling myself to my senses at last I raced down the stairs struggling out of my coat and when I reached Cora embraced her amidst it, hiding her among its folds. Instantly, she broke down weeping. "We don't have much time left," she said.

"Poor, bedeviled thing," I said.

"Oh you don't understand!" she said. "Of course, you never really have. You must," she paused a beat, "take me. And you must do it here and now."

"Lady Cora, please," I said and tried to lift her face toward mine. But she wouldn't allow me and kept her head lowered. I said to her gently, "You must stop this now."

"You don't understand! You don't know!" she repeated, again and again in a gathering frenzy, and I gathered her tighter beneath my greatcoat as the clock started up again, tolling absurdly. Then she said, "Do you hear it? We don't have much time!"

"My dear girl, I am affianced. And anyway it lowers you. It lowers—both of us," I said.

Here she raised her face toward mine, battered, pale and slick with tears. "If you took me and I took you, it would not want you then, you see. It only wants those, in that way, who are pure."

"It?" I said.

"You remind me of him. You are kind, just like he was."

"To whom," I said, "do you refer?"

"Asa Langford," Cora said.

"*Mister* Langford?"

"Why of course."

"But he—your mother said he—"

"No. They only say that he did that. He was trying to help, he was trying to save me! And so they gave him…"

"Gave him, yes?" But Cora only shook her head. "Where are your mother and brother right now?"

"Those *things* aren't my mother and brother," she said.

The house gave a groan and we jumped, toe to toe, both of us grasping the baluster. "Whatever the case," I said, holding her shoulders and steadying her as I looked in her eyes, "I cannot do the thing you ask. I love my sweetheart, after all."

And I really did love her, I felt in that moment, Cordelia Bingham of Central Park South, with her smeared penmanship and her coiled Yankee chill and her hesitancy to be with me at all, for that *was* true love, wasn't it: the thought you might not be enough. To her, I had said, "Cordelia Bingham, would you do me the honor of being my wife?"

And she had said to me, "I might."

At the time, anyway, it had seemed good enough.

"If you cannot see what is healthy for you, then you must go right now," said Cora. She pulled me off the bottom step with such violence I stumbled and fell to my knees, but she jerked me upright and then over foyer where she pushed me, head thumping, against the front door. "How many times must I tell you to *go*!"

She pushed me again, head rebounding. I laughed. Though by now, you might guess, it was only from fear. The clock was tolling ceaselessly and the rushing was deafening, surging around us, as though tides of unpotable, sinister water were barreling between the walls. For argument's sake, I grabbed hold of the doorknob but when I engaged it its bearing was iron. "It seems to be," I faltered, "stuck."

"It's too late, it's too late," Cora babbled. "It's here."

I tried the knob again, the lock and then the both of them at once. "They're gummed up good, aren't they?" I said, brutalizing the pair of them. "Send for a locksmith!" I started to laugh again wildly, then stopped. The din of the house was too loud to ignore. I felt my eyes tracking the walls and the ceiling where the stone and the woodwork appeared to be warping.

"Not there." Cora's eyes grazed the ceiling. "Out there."

Rising slowly on my toes, I stared through the portal set high in the door.

The first thing I noticed of Underwood House had been the dry moat that enclosed the foundation yet only now did I discern, albeit foggily, its function. A tide of dark jelly was filling the moat in the reddening glare of the last of the light and rising at a shocking rate along its root-encrusted sides. I could tell it was jelly the way the light hit it, but also by the way it rose, churning and chunking and blubbering up. The jelly was dark, and yet semi-opaque, with a purplish hue, as of fish fathoms deep. A solid black network pervaded the mass, like a skeleton, say, or a network of roots that appeared to enable the jelly with movement, tendrils of it shooting past beneath the mass with every wave. Beneath the top layer I saw something floating that had, at some point, been a man, now just a corpse of hair and bone. And having seen one, I now saw more and more, dozens of corpses suspended throughout with the same ravaged aspect of semi-digestion, their half-eaten faces turned plaintively up like the faces of fisher-folk trapped under ice. And I thought I perceived moving up from the deep the contours of Sebastian's face and beneath him a pale blue emulsion of cloth that might've been one of my hostess' dresses, but the way that the twilight broke over the surface I could not have said for sure. "What is it?" I said.

Cora didn't respond. The citrusy smell was now so overpowering I gasped and retched and huffed my nose. "We are not safe so near to ground. I know a place upstairs," said Cora, trying to pull me from the portal.

Outside, the jelly topped the moat and then was sucked down all at once—corpses, dark jelly, root system and all disappearing along with the last of the light as though a drain beneath the moat had suddenly been vacuumed free. I let my gaze wander away from the moat, up the side of the house, past its friezes and brackets, all the way to the windows set under the Witch's Cap on Underwood's third and final floor and I thought that I saw for a flickering moment the shapes of two people who stood at the glass, a man and a woman, their hands raised in greeting, who seemed to see me there below them. The sudden vision iced my blood. But when I looked closer so as to discern the faces of Sebastian and his mother, the living doppelgängers of the people in the jelly, the window glass was clear again. Cora Underwood said, "Flee with me, Mr. Lillie."

"But it's gone now," I heard myself saying aloud. "It was here for a moment but now it's…"

"Just starting." She grabbed my hand and pulled me with her. She was terribly strong, she would not be resisted. We took the grand staircase by threes. "That thing that you saw in the moat," she called back, "was only a part of it—only its mantle. It uses that to push itself up through the center of the house."

"*Inside* the house?"

"It is the house."

Getting my mind around that one, I stumbled "How many…" We rounded the bend in the stairs and I skidded a little, intent to catch up. Cora held my coat about her. "How many men have you managed to save?"

"You," she said, "will be my first."

When we reached the top stair, we paused there for a moment, watching the foyer below us for movement. I could go with her now or elect not to go. All that hung in the balance, of course, was my life.

The thing in the walls must've gathered itself, because down in the foyer it poured from the flues and welled up dark between the boards. At first it resembled the fluid I'd seen—or thought I had seen—Cora drink from the walls, but as it accrued in the chamber below it began to take on a more definite mass, growing up upon itself in wobbling and hideous tiers of dark matter before tumbling down from the top of the heap, this tumbledown forming a clutter of dark that spread along the foyer's floor. The mangled corpses I had seen suspended in the house's moat were nowhere to be found inside. That part of the creature, as Cora had said, only served as a muscle to push up the rest, its main body mass rushing up from the bottom. "We must hurry," said Cora. "There isn't much time."

"Hurry *where?*" I might've screamed.

The dark jelly was rising fast. The foyer was fifteen feet deep in the stuff with bits of it clinging midway up the stairs. Midway down the hall Cora dropped to all fours to get at something in the wood. The jelly thundered underfoot and I saw it creep onto the bend in the hall, seeping up the flock paper with a crackling sound that made runs in my stomach. Cora had opened a hidden compartment, a crawlspace set into the base of the wall. She gestured for me to get down on my knees and work my way inside. I balked. "Does it fill the whole house?" I asked, stooping to look.

The space was very tight indeed. Unhygienic-looking nails poked down from the beams.

"Every crevice and cranny save this one," said Cora.

"But that cannot be more," I peered, "than four or five square feet of space."

"You will enter first," she said, "and I will close the door behind."

"Nonsense," I said and stood back, waiting for her. I knew what she was going to do. I saw it in her panicked eyes, in the tremor of terror at her lip—how for so long she'd stayed here in Underwood House with these creatures no longer her mother and brother who had used her as bait to lure so many men, pure men like me and Mr. Langford, not one of whom Cora was able to save, and here Cora had had enough. The crawlspace could not fit us both. She deftly worked her way inside. She planned to lure me in with mercy and when I was safe to save none for herself. "Mr. Lillie," she urged. But I did not back down. "Mr. Lillie," she said, "I alone know the catch."

By way of an answer, I stood resolutely. "Never in my life," I said.

One summer out walking the Park with Cordelia, a severe thunderstorm had come up out of nowhere. We had not had umbrellas with us and nowhere near to run for dry so we ended up racing instead through the Park. We were bound for Fifth Avenue, half a mile east. Between the parkland and the street, a deluge of rainwater rushed by our toes. Some fruit-seller's boxes of slatted pine-board had been broken apart and abandoned nearby, and with hardly a thought I availed myself of them, getting down in the deluge, which lashed at my calves, and made for Cordelia an impro-vised bridge by which she was able to gain the concrete. For the rest of the day as we marched through Manhattan, my trousers and my shoes were soaked, and yet it was nothing compared to the joy of insuring Cordelia was happy and dry. It seemed miraculous to me so small an act could mean so much.

Too fast for her to block my way, I shut the crawlspace door on Cora. The catch wasn't nearly as hard as she claimed—the slide of a bolt and the flip of a latch. I could hear her fists hitting the wood from inside. I looked for other means of egress. There were small casement windows set high in the wall, just wide enough for Ethelred, and as the jelly filled the hall, smacking and groaning along the wainscoting and billowing over the ceiling like smoke, I wondered absentmindedly where the little old creature had got off to now.

I considered the letters I had in my coat. I knew that they contained no truth; they were courtship cantatas, the flimsiest stuff—engineered to please Cordelia, the partners of Bingham & Haverhill House. But the pitiful, glorious thing, I now realized, was that I had meant every word.

Thirty feet below the window and ten feet across lay the now empty moat whence the jellyfish creature, whatever it was, had pushed itself up to inhabit the house, and Cora was hammering now on the door, cursing me to let her out. The air was cold against my skin as I opened my fist and the letters fanned out, the first and perhaps the last time, I now realized, that since my arrival I'd set foot outside. As Underwood House crept up over my shoes I prayed that the letters would reach the far shore if only to show them, when living resumed, that I had been well worth the wait.

THE MAN WHO WORE DEATH

There once was a man who wore high khaki pants and button-up shirts with the faintest blue stripes. To say he was ugly would be to belie the fact that he was nondescript. His eyes were dull. His chin was weak. His hair was nut-brown, or jet-black, or straw-colored. His physique was lumpen. His posture was slack. His ears fit closely to his skull. In fact, the man was and he needed to be the most nondescript man among all those that breathed because he was an emissary of the force that had come to be known in this world and personified, mythically speaking, as Death.

Or rather not an emissary.

The word functionary might better explain the role this man played in relation to Death.

For the man here described, who had no proper name, was all but a cog in the bureaucracy that Death had developed to harvest the living.

If you'd happened to catch him abroad in the street in a north-eastern city, let's say, in the winter—and you wouldn't have noticed him, *ever*, we're sure, that's just how nondescript he was—but if you had noticed him, only this once, standing in line for a movie, per-haps and if you had happened to brush up against him, you'd have felt that his clothes were not fabric but flesh. He did not wear the clothes, he was them—a patterned complexion that coated his body.

You would wonder about him: how is he not cold, this uniquely unhandsome though not ugly man in his pouched business casual, standing so still?

How is his shoulder so soft to the touch?

How is his breath even faintly not smoking?

Where have I seen him before? you might ask.

Unless the man had come for you.

Here was the thing about Death's functionaries.

Like any good bureaucracy—or good bureaucracy in theory—the one overseen by the force known as Death was geared for peak efficiency. For Death, you see, had grown fatigued of meting out lifelessness day after day. Not least problematic was all of the plead-ing, the rending of hair and the wringing of hands, the appeals to a god that made Death belly-laugh. And when the appeals petered out and they did—Death's laugh had that effect on people—the vacuum of cold, life-renouncing despair that descended on people before they succumbed. Death was fatigued because Death was stretched thin across too many places and timeframes at once. And though Death might laugh, Death was not unaffected; cumulatively, the despair weighed on Death. The situation was untenable. Death could not perform Death's work.

And so Death created the bureaucracy that made death-enforcement a lesser ordeal, with its complex assignment of Death's functionaries to help in Death's enormous work. She'd birthed them from beneath Her robes, each one in his casing of unlovely clothing, each one with his features that mirrored the next if only in their incompleteness and off the functionaries went in their radial columns of disparate and few to accomplish the work to which Death was averse. No one among them was aware of the one set behind or before him in line and in this way they marched as a senseless brigade.

A seething dark net that enveloped the world.

Death was not a queen or an empress, per se, but a Grand Secretary who answered to no one.

Her main provision being this: Death alone could confer active death on the living.

But say that he had come for you—the man who wore death, in the northeastern city, outside of the theater, standing in line.

He would not have been wearing the high khaki pants and the button-up shirt with the faintest blue stripes. He would've been wearing your death yet to come.

That death—*your* death—would keep him warm.

You're standing in that movie line. You're twenty-one or twenty-two. While you're standing there, waiting, you're wooing your date, or

you're joking around with your two closest friends, or you're bathing your face in the warmth of the light streaming down from the bulbs of the movie marquee, a solitary moviegoer, glad to spend two hours alone. You notice that sitting before you in line and roughly level with your chest is a woman in a wheelchair with an oxygen tank, plastic tubes snaking around to the front. The tank is emitting a thin rhythmic breathing—in and out, out and in. Every time the tank expels the marquee sign appears to pulse. The wheelchair is facing the front of the line so you can't see the face of the lady inside, but you can see the back of her uncovered head: patched in places, tawny, hunched. It is very cold out. You can see she is smoking. How can she be smoking with oxygen flowing without blowing up on the spot? But she is. The smoke fumes up around her and into the light where the light of the sign seems to burn it away.

A feeling comes over you—brief, fragmentary.

Looking down at the sick woman's head, you think: *soon.*

Such thoughts do not stay with you long. You never see the woman's face. Some part of you never forgets her, however: her mostly bald head and her oxygen tank; her hunched-up nape; her plastic tubes. You know that she has lung cancer. And you know it is curdling into her slowly, filling her absences, blooming like coral.

What you don't know, at least not then, is one day you will have it too, and after a gross and prolonged struggle with it you will die like the woman you once saw in line.

Yet on the day that you do die and likely in the days before it, there will exist a part of you that does not struggle with your death, that does not plead with Death for mercy. A resignation grows in you from what had been the smallest seed.

Only now you remember the shape of her head.

Only now you remember yourself thinking: *Soon.*

Only now you remember the feeling you felt: *one day, perhaps, that will be me.*

And now Death comes for you with ease. She will not see you clutch at life. She will not be exhausted by mortal travails. In Her endless white robes She will light upon you from the place where She roams between myriad worlds and Her pale vestments will unravel around you, blinding you, eating you, wrapping you up. No one can say what lives under Death's robes, not even Her legion and cowed functionaries, who were born into being from under their folds.

But Death is a woman. Of this, they are sure.

For otherwise, how would they be?

She is only and utterly made of Her robes, the hollows of them whipping past you. They are not black—the stuff of myth—but blindingly, pristinely white. She descends in a gale of them. Shapely, totemic. She is glad for the way that you do not resist. It allows Her to gather the last of Her train and do what She is made to do.

And so we return to the man in the pants and the button-up shirt with the faintest blue stripes. For back in the northeastern city in winter, back when you were still alive, the woman in the wheelchair with the breathing apparatus is not in the crowd when the movie lets out and for an instant you accept this, assuming she went out the wheelchair exit or is waiting inside for the theater to clear. You go through the doors with your date or your friends or your self, no one else, feeling calm and renewed, and you walk down the curb and off into the night.

You never even see him there, underdressed and alone in the

dark and the cold. He stands parallel to the theater exit, the door swinging open to hide him, reveal him.

With his closely set ears and his hatchet-wound chin and his lank indeterminate pateful of hair, he may not even be to you, though you'd never remark it, a flesh and blood person. The man is—the man was, not a moment ago, the way that you were going to die. A taste of death coming up sour in your mouth so when the real thing came, you'd know it.

Here is a list of the things he remembered:

He remembered approaching an offshoreman's door in the clerical black of a policy agent and trying to pitch him the company plan that would pay out his family in case of his death, preparing the man for the moment, years later, drilling some wetlands in south Mississippi, when the rig he was working exploded and sank due to what would be deemed a "pneumatic malfunction."

He remembered becoming a flock of dark birds that lit on the eaves of a house in the suburbs above where a pilot of passenger jets had sat drinking coffee alone in his kitchen, prefiguring the accident which, only a year from that day, would occur when a similar flock would divert from its course and self-immolate in his airplane's right engine, plunging the vessel into the Pacific, killing everyone on board.

He remembered manifesting as a stab of indigestion on the Fourth of July at a neighborhood picnic, doubling over a boy in a blue camper chair as the fireworks finale swam big in his eyes now dimly aware that, five years in the future, he would die in a hail of policemen's gunfire, the sound of the bullets like Palms and Peonies, the blood spraying from him like sparks in the sky.

He remembered becoming a sonogram wave in the full uterus of a soon-to-be-mother, an erratic heartbeat that would spike and subside one month before the daughter's birth and signaling to her the marvelous world which lay beyond her mother's skin she'd enter as a lifeless thing, her mother's cord around her neck.

But he didn't stop there. He could never seem to. The man who wore death had a curious streak and it caused him to do the most curious things. For after every harbinger, when the people he'd marked had returned to their lives, he watched them for a little while in his high khaki pants and his button-up shirt.

He watched the offshoreman go back through his house and he watched him still closer as night took the swamp, resting a palm on his daughter's forehead, drinking a beer with the fridge door still open, making love to his wife with the lights bright as day, the only lit window in all of the house.

He watched the boy leaving the holiday picnic with the blue camper chair cradled under his arm and he watched him walk home through the blued, smoky air to the split-level house where he lived with his mother, carrying with him one last firework that he had saved for just this moment, and he lit it alone in the empty, dark street, the boy crying out while pin-wheeling in circles.

The man who wore death didn't know why he watched. He had thought that, perhaps, in the wake of his work the people would look different to him—more blessed among creatures, more brightly themselves. Some acknowledgement, maybe, of how life was brief in how they moved through time and space. Some hint of frightened need in them that would signal the man who wore death who they were.

For as long as the man who wore death had been there, he had only just once seen another one like him.

He had seen her while leaving a large hospital where the man who wore death had been putting in work—where in fact he had put on the sonogram wave that broke upon the baby girl. He almost didn't see her pass going in through the doorway as he was just leaving. He didn't know her by her looks or by her smell or by her gait but because of the fact that he couldn't have known her—because the woman was not there.

She'd been wearing a heather-grey pantsuit with pumps, her stature neither tall nor short and her face had been one of profound incompleteness, the bones without contour, the skin undercooked. He had grown so accustomed to seeing his subjects in all of their freckled particular meat that the sight of the woman who also wore death had profoundly unnerved him—seemed almost grotesque.

They watched each other for a while, pursuing their errands in different directions.

He had never seen anyone like her again.

Now the man who wore death felt initiative stirring.

He was on a nice street in a nice neighborhood where a ten-year-old boy would be riding his bike. It was autumn outside—early autumn and chilly. Leaves coated the street and fell down through the trees. The silly romantic aroma of woodsmoke. Life continued not without him, but in spite of the fact he had always been there.

The man stood at an intersection, just upon the sidewalk there and was wearing, as always, the high khaki pants and the button-up shirt with the faintest blue stripes.

He'd meant to manifest that day as a brake-cable fluke in the ten-year-old's bike, amounting to a breathless swerve in the path of a number of slow-moving cars, guaranteeing that twenty-five years from that day, side-swiped and killed by an off-duty cab, he would not exhaust Death with his sadness and terror when the thought out of nowhere came to him: *of course.*

That ten-year-old was coming, now.

No longer a man but a brief disconnect between the lever and the brakes, the man who wore death infiltrated the bike.

The ten-year-old boy on the bike pedaled harder, his torso bent over the top of the frame. The cars came on. The brakes gave out. The bike began to swerve away. Yet instead of absenting himself from the bike and taking his post up again on the curb, the man who wore death festered deep in the frame.

And then there was no going back.

As the boy jackknifed over the top of the hood, his head snapped up against his chest and the top of his spinal cord snapped in two pieces. He somehow subsided on top of the hood, one arm hanging over the driver's side window, blood yo-yoing down from his hand to the street where it pattered and set near the tire. Glops of blood escaped his mouth. A young woman sat at the wheel of the car with two small daughters in the back. One was older, facing forward, the other one younger and still in a car-seat and the two of them, too, began yelling and sobbing while clutching at each other's arms. A man from a house on the block got there first and lifted the dead boy off the hood. Other mothers and fathers, and sisters and brothers emerged in a throng from the neighboring houses while the first man, who'd lifted the boy from the hood, now laid him out upon some grass.

That was when something unheard of took place.

The crowd of people leaned away. The child's broken body was rising again: his bloodstained and angelic mouth. His bruised and cluttered limbs. His eyes. The links in the boy's shattered neck were correcting. His breath traveled from him in great, gummy rasps. He was popping his neck as he rose from the lawn like a welterweight boxer half-dead on his feet and the people lurched back to allow him this blessing, this requisitioned life, regained.

The resurrection came and went, but the man who wore death still remembered the boy.

He remembered, of course, the reanimate limbs and how red blood had stained the mouth, but he also remembered the cries of the children .(*Just like Jesus! Just like Jesus!*) The fathers' violent gasps and sobs. The serene, faintly puzzled expression of joy on the faces of mothers, reduced to her knees. He might've only swerved the bike before righting its course again (*might've,* but hadn't) and this had been the thing at last that would not let the boy stay dead.

The man who wore death had done Death's sacred work.

And then like a glitch in a programming system or an isolated ripple on the surface of a pond, death had smoothed itself over. Reversed, self-corrected.

There'd been no great unwinding of Death in Her robes that gathered him up into reckoning thunder. There'd been no reverse rapture that marked him alone, Death's voice, in the voice of a harpy, declaiming. There'd been no sign, no visitation.

Here were more miracles that the man brought about.

Instead of becoming a heavy nose bleed down the face of a boy at his grandfather's funeral—he was eating a cheese-stick amidst the reception—looking ahead to a heavier one when the boy over-dosed on cocaine at a party, dying on the bathroom floor, his limbs out-flung at thirty-six, the man who wore death had a different plan. He bloated to an aneurysm that stopped the boy's heart and collapsed him facedown, shattering the coffee table, a curtain of blood inundating his shirt. But then as his relatives crowded around him, touching his slippery face with their hands, he twitched his nose and raised his hand to brush the cheese-crumbs from his face.

Or.

Instead of becoming a wobbly stool where a bipolar stagehand was tying a noose for the climactic scene in a high school play, the sudden bucking of the stool beneath the swaying of the noose fore-telling the fact of her own suicide which she would enact, two years later, in college, the man who wore death had contrived otherwise. He made the bucking stool collapse, and the neck of the stage-hand get caught in the noose, and the noose toll with vigor above the footlights to the horror and trauma of everyone watching. But when her classmates took her down and laid her out upon the stage, the life that had fled her came flooding again and she lurched up among the small crowd that had gathered.

Or.

Instead of becoming a faulty crosstie in the path of an oncoming passenger train—the train had left New Orleans and was headed to Chicago—causing the train to go snaking insanely and prognosticating the various deaths of all the passengers onboard, the man who wore death acted out of impatience. He formed as a gap in the tracks up ahead and the train jackknifed out of alignment and flipped, the train's middle cars going end over end. The arms and legs of passengers sticking out of the windows that no longer were. The conflagration fires burned low and soon the survivors walked out of the smoke to stand around the mangled cars while out of them clambered the scorched and the bloodied, the twisted and torn, the impaled and on-fire. Yet as they dropped to earth again their depredations seemed to heal, their limbs growing back and their burns smoothing over while onlookers' eyes rolled up white in their heads.

He was more in these moments than one functionary enacting the work of the Grand Secretary but a creature of influence, spirit, conviction. In some ways he even resembled a man. And every man, he felt, was different.

He had seen them drink beer with the fridge door still open and he had seen them love their wives. He had seen them rotate in the dark air of evening, sparks shooting out the ends of their hands.

The deaths he made were more than deaths. They were a form of earthly grace.

And he grew, in a manner, addicted to grace, to the weird

miracles that he caused to occur and when he did not make them so he shook inside his skin of clothes.

Yet the man who wore death nursed his cravings in secret. Nobody was witness for nobody saw him. And the man who wore death had occasion to doubt: had they been miracles at all?

A couple weeks later he found himself trekking a mountainous region in deep winter snow. The sky was as polished and hard as a grave. The man who wore death wore his high khaki pants and his button-up shirt with the faintest blue stripes but nothing else of extra warmth and these were suited to his needs.

He was there on an errand as Death's functionary, tracking a man on his climb to the top. The man was a famous and skilled mountaineer who had climbed in his lifetime a good many peaks. This would've been another one were it not for the man who wore death on his trail, anonymous amidst the snow, continuing on when the mountaineer rested.

Though distant by hundreds of yards from the climber, the man who wore death was beginning to change. The treacherous rock-slide would only just miss them. Right before it reached the men, it would hit on a broad ledge of stone just above them and would go pouring past them, life-hungry and fluid, and the climber would know by it two decades later that men such as him cheated Death only once.

But the man who wore death knew he wouldn't stop there.

In other words, he knew full well he would bully them all from the edge of the pass, and he would be down in the snowfields again when they startled up mangled and rimed in cold blood. He would witness the new virgin breaths that they took, pluming in the winter air.

The man who wore death had been climbing the mountain just behind the mountaineer.

By midday, they were more than halfway to the top. And since the man who wore death had his miracle planned for some time in the realm of dusk, with the mountaineer cloudy and tired from his labors, he figured he had time enough to stop for a moment and look at the stars. He wasn't human, this was true, but had often been moved and transfixed by earth's beauty. He had even had cause to stand trembling before it: the way that twilight mutes and glares through the curtains of moss overhanging a river. The way that a valley with green humps and peaks will be woven among its depressions with fog. Now he lay on his back on the densely packed snow and watched newer snow falling out of the sky and beyond it the stars in their icy precision. The man who wore death hardly noticed at first when a strip of white cloth brushed the tip of his nose.

A figure descended from out of the greyness. She was cloaked in white robes from Her toes to Her head, and the robes surged around Her like something alive, and She rushed past the eyes of the man who wore death for what seemed like a hundred feet, Her mantle of white desolation unending pouring down around him where he lay in the snow.

As the Grand Secretary unraveled around him, the world before him seemed to change. His view of the branches, the snow and the stars was on fire at the edges with tongues of white cloth. He felt his blood, if blood he had, repolarize and change its course. Now cycling through him was some other substance, not life-giving fluid but vast information, a list of the dying and soon-to-be-dead which was actually every last name on the planet, the numberless Rolls of the Grand Secretary, and now he alone among Death's functionaries could say what lived beneath the robes.

And he realized that over this surfeit of time of causing his weird miracles to occur, he had never once asked himself why he had done it. To be closer to human, perhaps there was that, though the man who wore death knew he'd never be human. So perhaps to distinguish himself in some way—to do things that Death would be forced to undo. To prove that he himself was different in the scheme of Death's legion and cowed functionaries, that he was more than just a cog—that he, too, had the power to make or unmake. He had done it for so many very good reasons apart from the will of the Grand Secretary but now as She settled around him whole cloth he saw the opposite was true.

He had done it for Death: Her regard, Her approval. And that need on his part had proved he was a cog, had proved that he'd accomplished nothing. For his efforts, he'd not be rewarded but punished by becoming much more than the man who wore death but the Grand Secretary Herself, pouring on him, the names engulfing him like flies. There was finally no one else but Her. He saw he could be no one else.

He felt himself lifting along with the robes until he was floating above the expanse. The shape of the man in the high khaki pants and the button-up shirt with the faintest blue stripes was hollowed in the snow below, new snowfall beginning to blur him already.

Through the white agonies of the robes he saw this: the way down the mountain, tree-mottled and steep. A skinny old woman in nothing but rags was walking downhill through the onrushing snow. Her head was cowled against the cold and she took the hill slowly, arms crooked at her sides, the ends of the arms poking out of the rags as frail and luminous as bone. He could see she was old, very old, close to death. Her breath smoked in the winter air. And though he could not see her face, her movements bespoke a profound apprehension, like an old woman crossing an iced-over pond in the knowledge this step or the next one will take her.

She would not last out here for long.

The man who was Death felt the robes warming to him, conforming themselves to his torso and limbs. The woman stopped walking, turned halfway around. There in the dark of her cowl she stood, waiting.

THE CASE OF THE AIR-DANCER

STRANGE ENCOUNTERS
Season 3, Episode 9
"The Case of the Air-Dancer"

[Intro Theme: Theremin, spare piano]

There is limitless strangeness at large in our world... [shadowy shape sliding under the water] [clown laughing in darkened room]... Few of us will ever glimpse it [yellow cat's eye flashes open] Strange Encounters shines a light... [cat eye's pupil widens, brightens, revealing the show's title card in green letters]... into all of the world's corners better left dark...

MARISSA
DEVIN'S CHILDHOOD BEST FRIEND

I guess I should just start with Devin. This all happened our sophomore year. He'd had a rough summer, his dad gone a lot, just him and his mom all alone in the house. Devin started to do what he wanted to do. He started to wear what he wanted to wear. Nail polish, a little mascara, but subtle. And sometimes, I guess, he wore blouses to school or these garments that might've been blouses or shirts. Me and him we would go and shop for them together. Claire's, Forever 21. First day of school he wore this new one, yellow with slices of red watermelon. It was pretty damn cute! He was proud of that shirt. He wore it, probably, twice a week. For the assholes at school that was two days too much.

LEILA
DEVIN'S MOM

Devin was quiet the summer before but twice as quiet in the fall. Always it was him and Marissa out rambling but sometimes they sat long enough to eat something. That girl was always here for dinner. She was one of those, what's the phrase, latch and key kids? Her and Devin loved each other. Been friends since the seventh or eighth grade, I think. He had no other friends that I knew of from school. I sort of blame myself, I guess? Not for what happened, I couldn't control that, but Chase was gone a lot that fall. Pharma runs—mostly the Midwest and places. Him and Devin had zero and then some in common, but we all made it work and I guess that was love.

SHERIFF VAUGHN
CHIEF INVESTIGATING OFFICER

This show's about the murders, right? Logan Orvis went missing on Halloween night. Next morning his mom called us down at the station. It was good that she did that, we all agreed then, because early like that it can still make a difference but after that it's pretty grim. That day passed and then another. I think we were all busy chasing down leads. We thought he'd run off with his girlfriend or something. Knocked her up, maybe. Lit out for the next place. That happens sometimes to the kids in this town. When we didn't find him, the search parties started, but I guess by that point he was already gone.

RIDONKULOUS RICK
OWNER OF RIDONKULOUS RICK'S AUTOS

The Devin kid, yeah, I mean what can you say? Nice kid, polite. A little queer. But folks gone do what they gone do. And sure, he came here sometimes, yeah. Mostly when the lot was closed. I own the place but hey, so what? You can't control who comes and goes and the kid never struck me as much of a threat. He'd just stand in the dark, staring at the air-dancer. In the back of the dealership I had my office but back where I sat you could see clear across to the window that looked on the lot and the street. I was drinking a lot then. Real late hours at work. Sorry, Sarah Beth, Luanne! I'm sober now—my twelve-year chip. But the Devin kid, yeah, he would come here at night, staring up at the air-dancer, covered in makeup. [commentary off-camera] An air-dancer, you know, it's one of those figures? About twenty feet with the goofy-ass smile that some folks use for advertising, runs on an electric fan? You set it up close to the front of your place to lure in business from highway. Also heard them called tube men or tall boys and such, but air-dancer always made most sense to me. Ours was purple. Real nice fella! Little spiky head of hair. Even named him Twisty—ha!

And believe you me, brother, them shits are expensive. The Devin kid, he seemed to love it. I guess they had, like, some connection. I remember that one time he came in a dress! Another in cutoffs, this little blue tube-top. He liked to play dress up and have the thing watch. The first night I saw him, like, what's this kid doing? But after that I didn't care. Here in my office, him standing out there, it almost got to be this comfort.

JACQUI ORVIS
LOGAN ORVIS' MOTHER

My sweet boy Logan was the first. It's been twelve years. I miss him lots.

LEILA
DEVIN'S MOM

Devin came home beat that year. Every evening sulky, quiet. Marissa was still coming over for dinner but she was weird and quiet, too. Almost like they had this secret, though it was more than that with Devin. Bruises up and down his arms. A black eye once. Him walking funny. I'd ask him, "Baby, what is that?" But he would only chew his food.

MARISSA
DEVIN'S CHILDHOOD BEST FRIEND

Logan Orvis, all those dudes, they were totally horrible bullies to Devin. They'd see him coming down the hall, not strutting his stuff but just walking along, and they'd slam him against it, like, hitting the lockers. One time they punched him in the stomach. They'd say terrible shit to him. "Cocksucker!" "Shit-stick!" That went on for a little while. Then it started to get way more dangerous—private. Them cornering Devin in parts of the school where they knew no one else would be and smacking his ass-cheeks so hard they left bruises. Bitch-slapping him—"Take it!"—and twisting his nipples. Ramming their hands up the crotch of his pants and squeezing around up there: "What you got going?" This was real prosecutable, sexual stuff. I was always a tomboy. An indoor kid, too. Liked plays and movies, reading books. That's how me and Devin first bonded, I guess. But I knew from my time being bullied by girls in middle school and in the streets that you just had to step to them, show them your stuff. Devin didn't even try. He would slide to the floor and hunch down in this ball, his arms clutching his knees—oh, boy. These kids were Great Whites. They smelled blood in the water. And Devin was floating there, letting them bite.

SHERIFF VAUGHN
CHIEF INVESTIGATING OFFICER

We found the Orvis kid—November? I'm pretty sure it was November. A few days after Halloween. There were still pumpkins rotting on everyone's porch.

JACQUI ORVIS
LOGAN ORVIS' MOTHER

My grandpa owned a slaughterhouse. I watched them do it all the time. Put the cows inside these stalls. Come up with the bolt gun and, *pffft*, it's lights out. After they would hack it up and grind the meat for chuck and such. That's how they found Logan. Just chuck and ripped fabric. A couple bones, maybe, but there wasn't much.

MARISSA
DEVIN'S CHILDHOOD BEST FRIEND

I should probably get to the air-dancer, right? Devin loved that goddamned thing! The first time he took me to see it—September? All day on the weekends we did what we wanted and most of the time also into the night. Sometimes we'd go to this little graveyard right out on the edge of town and we'd smoke cigarettes on the headstones, goof off. Knock on the graves, like, hello there, how's death? Other times we would wander the streets on our own. One night we wound up at Ridonkulous Rick's and I thought when we got there, it just seemed so random, we were going to do something to one of the cars. Key it, maybe. Punch the tires. But Devin just stopped out in front of the lot. Air-dancer was up there, right next to the sign. Dancing crazy in the breeze. Thin arms and the tube of its body, that's all, mounted on some kind of motor. [commentary off-camera] Huh. A fan. I never knew that, all these years. I have this theory—want to hear it? [commentary off-camera] It's nothing profound, only that in this world there are two kinds of people—those that see an air-dancer and it just sort of blends with the scenery, right? But that can never happen with the other kind of person. They see one and they can't stop looking. Gooseflesh, like someone walked over their grave, and their mind begins shouting: *Nope! Nope-ity nope!* I'm that second kind, okay? But I don't think I knew till I saw one up close. Devin, he was hypnotized. He seemed to see it like some god. Or like his copilot through life, or whatever. "It's beautiful, isn't it, Missy?" Okay. "It's free," Devin said.

"It just goes with the breeze." Now I wonder if he knew about the fan either.

RIDONKULOUS RICK
OWNER OF RIDONKULOUS RICK'S AUTOS

Sometimes he'd bring that girl with him. What was her name again? Misty? Michelle? [answer off-screen] Marissa, right. I almost went out there once, told them to get, but then I figured, what's the problem? Admiring my business flair might teach them something. Now I wish that I'd gone out.

LEILA
DEVIN'S MOM

Mid-October, this one night, Devin comes home and runs straight to this room. Not even a, "Hey, mom," just in, like a shot, and I got off the couch and I knocked on his door. I don't remember what I said. Probably something like, "Baby, what's wrong? Whatever it is it's not that bad." But it *was* bad, we know that now. [closes eyes] Just really bad.

MARISSA
DEVIN'S CHILDHOOD BEST FRIEND

Logan Orvis. Peter Sykes. Jonathan Maybrook. Martin Steenbergen. You don't forget assholes like that. Especially after what they did to Devin after health class that day in the locker room showers. We didn't have sex-ed, go figure, but we did have health class, bundled in with PE. Mister Peachtree, the teacher,

Coach Peachtree we called him, would put up transparency slides of our bodies and show us the various parts with his pointer. Testes, shaft, you know the drill, and those boys would go fucking nuts! "Donkey dick," they'd yell. "Jizz blaster!" And this one day in class, right before Halloween, after Coach had explained to us how babies happened with the vag on one side and the dick on the other, Logan Orvis yelled, "Like Devin! Devin's got both of those, he can make babies!" Half of the class laughed but most of them didn't. Like I said, Devin's strategy up until then was just to keep sitting there quiet and passive but when Logan said that he seemed to wake up. He threw his pencil straight at Logan. Fucking beautiful shot! [commentary off-camera] Sorry, sorry, sailor's mouth, but the pencil, it hit Logan right in the face. Below his left eye, drew a little blood even. The class went nutso! Coach went, "Chill." Then we suited for gym and they ran us around. And only later, in the showers, according to Devin and why would he lie? Logan and Peter and Johnny and Martin surrounded Devin in his stall. The boys were naked. So was Devin. "Got any more lead in that pencil dick, faggot?" Two of them grabbed him to keep him from moving. Then one by one they, you know—well. Can I say what they did to him? [answer off-camera] They held him there standing beneath the gym shower and forced his penis in their mouths. Like sucking him off one by one, but real rough. Scratching and biting and shouting filth at him. And this is awful, really, gah, which Devin only told me later but being, like, a teenage boy, as he was then so who can blame him, Devin could feel himself getting aroused. That only made them louder, meaner. "You like that, huh, faggot? You like that?" they said. And Devin was just so ashamed. Where *the fuck* was Coach Peachtree? I'm sorry, it's just…

SHERIFF VAUGHN
CHIEF INVESTIGATING OFFICER

Kids are cruel sometimes, you know? But it's hard to prove bullying actually *happened*. Try a decade ago with these kids running wild and most of them don't even own a computer. But lots of people back it up, this Devin kid's story of what they did to him, what they had been doing to him all that year. This isn't the bible, though. This is the law. Two wrongs never make a right. Three wrongs even less of one. So I'm saying, yeah, they were rotten mean kids, but that doesn't mean they deserved what they got. Even less when you look at the way that they died.

RIDONKULOUS RICK
OWNER OF RIDONKULOUS RICK'S AUTOS

Halloween was cold that year. I had to go hard on the scotch to stay warm. Devin and Marissa, they showed up that night, standing out on the street looking up at old Twisty, and that night he was really going! Halloween, so the kids were in costumes, of course. At first it was tricky to see who they were. The girl, Marissa, dressed like Jason. Jumpsuit, hockey mask, fake knife. The Devin kid dressed like—Vampirella? Morticia Addams? Someone like that. He was wearing this long slinky black evening gown. Long black wig, this pancake makeup. Both kids knelt in front of Twisty like he might be some goofy God or one of God's creatures possessed by the Devil and they were, like, going to offer him something, see if he could sort them out. The Devin kid got out this paper, a printout of something with words written on it, but I was too far off to see what it was and then they were passing it back and forth, reading. Shouting words up at Twisty out there in the cold.

MARISSA
DEVIN'S CHILDHOOD BEST FRIEND

Can people manifest revenge? Like, out of their bodies? Some kind of blunt force? Devin could. At least, I think. His body had never been his—*felt* like his—and that's how he did it, I think, with that pain. It sure as hell wasn't the spell that we found while surfing revengehex.com, or whatever. "Trespass against trespass, an eye for an eye, vouchsafe my vengeful arrow fly..." But when Devin read it, his parts of the script, he really seemed to feel the words. He read it in this trembling voice. We passed the printout, taking turns, looking up at that air-dancer swaying above us. It was smiling down at us. It never stopped smiling, and in between its rows of teeth this giant gap of solid black. And I remember wondering if you punctured that part of the air-dancer's mouth would the whole thing deflate or, like, would it keep dancing? When we finished the spell, we read their names.

RIDONKULOUS RICK
OWNER OF RIDONKULOUS RICK'S AUTOS

I'm not sure what I saw that night. See my little office where I had been drinking was in back of the place, behind the floor. When I was there at night alone I always kept the door wide open, letting the office light shine on the floor in case someone tried to break in or boost cars, but even through the open door, it's hundreds of feet to the front of the place. And then it's another, say, five hundred feet through the lot to the air dancer, out on the street. I didn't see something so much as two things that taken together add up to a third one. Air-dancer was up there. And then it was gone. Now I said I'd been drinking, but *come the fuck on.*

SHERIFF VAUGHN
CHIEF INVESTIGATING OFFICER

When something that horrible happens to kids in a town of our size, people see what they want to. Some folks lost their minds with grief. Others couldn't face the truth. I'm pretty sure I know what happened. And it wasn't some goddamn promotional prop possessed by some damn supernatural force. A person murdered those three kids. And twelve years out, we still know who.

JACQUI ORVIS
LOGAN ORVIS' MOTHER

Logan and all of them went trick-or-treating. That's what he told me anyway. But they were, what, 15, 16? I may be old but I'm not stupid. Boys that age say they're trick-or-treating you can bet that they're drinking or TP-ing houses. Logan had a werewolf mask on. All them boys were wearing masks. But masks for getting candy? Ha. Those masks were for not getting caught.

RIDONKULOUS RICK
OWNER OF RIDONKULOUS RICK'S AUTOS

No, I didn't call the cops. Feeling, I don't know, kind of Chuck Norris or something. Got straight in my car and went out to look for them, but when I found them not far off just walking along through the dark side by side, what was I going to accuse them of doing?

Ripping the air-dancer off of its fan-mount? Stashing it some place? Now, come on. I was also too drunk to keep driving by that point. Went on home to get some sleep. But then when I came to the lot the next morning, old Twisty was standing back up on his mount.

MARTIN STEENBERGEN
VICTIM

Mind if I smoke? [answer off-camera] Been a while since I talked about all of this stuff. Guess Halloween night is the best place to start. Went on a couple pumpkin raids. Put some KB in the air, you know, baby. Crushed a twelver of Ice at the old middle school, Logan, me, Johnny and P-Psyche—the boys. They're all dead now, you know that right? Me and Logan said, "Hey now, let's keep the buzz going!" Crushed our cans and set off walking. Across the playground, up the steps and over the football field toward the gas station. Midway across the field we stopped and Logan said, "You hear that, man?" I said, "Hear what?" He said, "That rustling." I said, "Boy!" But Logan just stood there all freaked and said, "Listen." I did hear it now, but it wasn't a rustling. It was more like a whistling or zipping sound, kind of. Like a silk parachute being dragged through the trees. And that's when we saw it against the moonlight, crawling out of the treeline behind the goalpost. All spindly and shit. And, like, dragging itself. Low down to the ground with these little thin arms. The rest of it, way longer, coming behind it. It didn't go around the goal like something normal might've done but climbed up and over it. Slithering, jerking. Its mouth stretching open with darkness inside. We wanted to run but we just stood there, frozen. By then it was already too late for Logan.

JACQUI ORVIS
LOGAN ORVIS' MOTHER

I called the cops November first. Close to two in the afternoon, as I remember. On the weekends he'd usually stay at a friend's house and you can bet on Halloween. I knew they slept late but this late was just crazy.

SHERIFF VAUGHN
CHIEF INVESTIGATING OFFICER

We found him by the trail of blood. I'd say like a slug's trail but it was more patchy. A little here, a little there, along the right side of the street in the gutter. Like someone had dragged the kid all of that way, shedding ground-up deposits of him as they went. Even now, looking back at crime scene forensics, I'm not really sure how the murderer did it or chose to do it that way, even. It was just so— bizarre. We'd find some in the gutter. More down in the sewer, then some in the street. The victim had been, we determined, chewed up by some large piece of farming machinery, maybe? The remains bundled up in a suitcase or sack and distributed over a pretty wide space—basically, one end of town to the other. Starting near the middle school, ending out near the car dealership near the highway. We had only one witness, the Steenbergen kid, and what he told us made no sense. The air-dancer did it! I mean, it's insulting. Drug-tested the kid after taking his statement and he'd been smoking dope all night. But he was the first one to start with that story and it caught on with certain people—Marissa and the Devin kid, though we know now they both had incentive to lie.

LEILA
DEVIN'S MOM

Marissa slept over on Halloween night. They'd been out trick-or-treating, a little old for it, but I figured at least they were having some fun. Chase was coming home—two days? I couldn't get to sleep that night, I hadn't been sleeping much those days and I don't think I heard them come in through the front, but maybe three or four a.m. I heard them still awake, still talking. I went to Devin's door and knocked. Told them it was time to gear down for the night. Past noon the next day when I went in to wake them they were still in their costumes, asleep on the floor.

MARISSA
DEVIN'S CHILDHOOD BEST FRIEND

When the air-dancer came down to hover before us, Devin dropped the revenge spell and it blew away. That's also when he reached his hand out, touched it right in that darkness that lived in its mouth.

JACQUI ORVIS
LOGAN ORVIS' MOTHER

Sorry. [commentary off-camera] I can't. Think I need to take a break.

RIDONKULOUS RICK
OWNER OF RIDONKULOUS RICK'S AUTOS

Sherriff Vaughn came here to question me first, the very same day that they found Logan Orvis. Good thing I had an alibi. I also told about the kids, Marissa and Devin, on Halloween night. You see, I was still scared they'd pin it on me. I never imagined they actually done it.

SHERRIFF VAUGHN
CHIEF INVESTIGATING OFFICER

And then, nearby, we found the list.

MARISSA
DEVIN'S CHILDHOOD BEST FRIEND

That's what they called it—a list, not a spell—when they brought us down to the station for questions. It said "Get Even Spell" at the top of the sheet, below that the text, the boys' names underneath it. We figured we might as well tell them the truth. Wasn't even, like, something we planned in advance. We came to it separately. Questioned us that way, off in different small rooms like they do in the movies. We told them the story of Logan and Johnny and Peter and Martin all hassling Devin and Devin even told them, too, that terrible thing that the boys had done to him after health class that day in the locker room showers. He couldn't have told Sherriff Vaughn the whole thing, not in the detail he told me before, but whatever he told him, it had Devin crying, half to remember and half from the shame and when Devin did that the Sheriff got awkward, turned his eyes from Devin's eyes. Muttered something weird to Devin that Devin thought might've been, "Boys can be fools," but then later on, maybe, "Boys will be boys." After that, Sheriff Vaughn just left the room and sent in a beat cop to finish the statement, and we both told the cops that we hadn't killed Logan because for all we knew we hadn't. What neither of us told them though was about how the air-dancer started to change—whirling around as we read through the spell before leaning down to us, floating there, waiting. I don't even think that *we'd* processed it yet or what it meant for Logan Orvis. After that, they let us go. The next day they found Peter Sykes.

LEILA
DEVIN'S MOM

Several days into all this, Chase came home. All that September he'd had a bad run. Pharma rep, that's what Chase did, which meant he was pretty much off on his own, and sure, there were a few good years when he would be out raking in the commissions, but all that luck was over now. Probably he was feeling scared about the winter months to come—how he would support us and be there at once. But then when I told him about what had happened, that a couple of guys had been hassling Devin and one of those guys had been horribly murdered and Devin, not the prime suspect, had been questioned about it and might see round two, he didn't run out and get drunk to forget like a lesser man might've. Chase wasn't like that. Not the world's most hands-on dad but good in a crisis. He said that he'd do anything to help Devin. He said that we needed to think up a plan.

RIDONKULOUS RICK
OWNER OF RIDONKULOUS RICK'S AUTOS

I was down at the office now most every night. Too drunk to drive home, I just crashed at my desk. Woke up in my office chair, mouth full of cat-shit. Partly because I had come to the point that you could've pushed me as light as a feather for me to end up in AA the next day and partly because after what I had seen, I more than half thought I was losing my mind and the scotch was the best way to quiet it, sort of, or make it so I wouldn't notice. That goddamned air-dancer out front of the lot! One night it was gone and then back the next morning. I thought that I should call the cops but I didn't know what the hell I would tell them.

MARTIN STEENBERGEN
VICTIM

Johnny heard from P-Syke last. Talking on the phone that night. They'd talk every night after school on the phone and Johnny was trying to talk P-Syke down after the bad shit that happened to Logan. P-Syke, he was sure we was cursed in some way. A curse that you catch like in some scary movie. And when he was talking with Johnny that night, he talked himself into a pretty tight corner, getting all 'noided out about him being next so P-Syke told Johnny he needed to blaze in the alley in back of his house to calm down. When P-Syke was out there, that's when it came for him. Him and Johnny had ended the phone call by then. But I think about that, what that must've been like, with the front of it filling the mouth of that alley, crouched there on its little arms and P-Syke knowing that thing, waiting there, was the last thing he'd see. Talk about a buzzkill man! We heard later on that he'd swallowed the blunt because the cops found it smushed up in his stomach.

MARISSA
DEVIN'S CHILDHOOD BEST FRIEND

When they found Peter Sykes scattered down in the sewer the same way they found Logan Orvis, me and Devin knew two things. First, Sheriff Vaughn wasn't done with us yet. Second, it was time to stop this. The hex or possession, whatever it was, seemed to be picking them off one by one. We remembered the order we'd spoken their names: Logan, Peter, Johnny, Martin. Basically the order of their awfulness to Devin beginning with Logan and ending with Martin. Johnny was the next in line. So that third night we told some lie about a late-night dress rehearsal, went down to Ridonkulous Rick's, waited for it. To reverse a revenge spell, we found out online, you had to burn the remnants of it, but Sherriff Vaughn still had the printout. So we printed the whole thing out again with the same four boys' names written on it and we had it with us, that night, down at Rick's. When the air-dancer started to change on its mount, this sort of, like, circular sway-ing, all woozy, with its long, skinny face grinning up at the stars, Devin read an incantation: "Trespasses pardoned, eyes restored, let vengeful poison flow no more…" I mean, who writes these Wiccan curses? I burned the printout while he said it. Maybe we should've used the first one. Or maybe Devin didn't mean it. Because after the spell's ashes floated away, the air-dancer lifted itself from its mount.

RIDONKULOUS RICK
OWNER OF RIDONKULOUS RICK'S AUTOS

Uh-huh, not cool! Not cool at all! When I saw that, man, I was done. I killed off the bottle of scotch I was drinking. I checked myself into a clinic that night.

JACQUI ORVIS
LOGAN ORVIS' MOTHER

With Logan dead and Peter too and then they found that awful list—a kill list, come on, I mean that's what it was, though for some reason nobody called it that then—why was nobody checking on Jonathan Maybrook? Because he was po trash, like us, and because in the end it was more about Devin. Protecting him, making sure *he* wasn't hurt, like he was the vulnerable one, not those boys.

MARISSA
DEVIN'S CHILDHOOD BEST FRIEND

To get out to Johnny's before the air-dancer, we took a shortcut through some yards. You see, it didn't move that fast, the way it dragged itself along, but when we got to Johnny's house he was out on his porch with a gun waiting for it. Johnny was a little sad. Not straight-up cruel like Pete and Logan or half-decent sometimes like Martin Steenbergen, but just, like, this doofus. A follower, putty. Drunken redneck mom and dad who were never around much and not that night, either. Waiting there on the porch to stand off with the thing was the most, like, original thought Johnny had but when me and Devin showed up on the steps, just trying to step in and handle it for him, well Johnny didn't want to hear it. He was crying all sloppy in only his undies. Spittle and drool coming out of this mouth. "Fucking queers, fucking freaks! Get the hell off my porch!" Okay, Johnny, much obliged. Johnny pointed the gun at us. Can you believe it? But we didn't need to do anything else because that's when the air-dancer came up behind us. We parted to let it crawl through the front yard and Johnny started firing at it but he was too nervous to do more than wing it. By then it was already climbing the porch.

SHERIFF VAUGHN
CHIEF INVESTIGATING OFFICER

Peter Sykes and Johnny Maybrook were found in a similar manner to Logan. Mutilated, masticated, what was left of them shoved down a series of drains. That's around when we started to get smart about it—too little, too late, lots of folks will still tell you, but we were in uncharted waters. We took a few samples of victims' remains, sent them off to a DNA lab in the city.

MARISSA
DEVIN'S CHILDHOOD BEST FRIEND

In grade school, we went to the zoo on a field trip. They let us watch them feed the snakes. The python's den was so, so dark. We were up on our tiptoes to get a look at it and then we saw this guinea pig that the trainers had with them come scrambling in. The python, bright yellow with swirly white stripes, had caught it squirming, still alive. Its mouth opened up and its jaw, like, unhinged, and the python deep-throated this guinea pig down. A little traumatic, you think? Kids were screaming. That's the way that it got Johnny.

162

JACQUI ORVIS
LOGAN ORVIS' MOTHER

You bet that I blame lots of people involved. Old Sheriff Due Process for not acting sooner, the folks at the school for not seeing the signs. Hell, even blame myself sometimes, even though I know I shouldn't. But most of all I blame that family. That goddamn space-case, crazy woman, not raising her boy right. Rude—just rude. Her pill-slanging husband, gone half of the year. Say what you will, if he'd been there more often, a family needs a man to run it. That Devin kid weren't growing into one right—prancing around in those dresses, mascara. They say the transgenders are like anyone but I don't subscribe to that, not for a second. They let them in the military. Let them go in whichever restroom they please. Let them do mostly whatever they want and what are we left with? A whole lotta nothing. If that screwed-up family had got itself right then those three boys would be alive.

LEILA
DEVIN'S MOM

Jacqui Orvis never liked me. This predates what happened to Logan and them but it wasn't bad as a handy excuse. She started her own little crusade against us. Calling our house at all hours of the night. Showing up on our doorstep to scream murder at us. Chase finally said if she didn't back off he'd have her arrested and that calmed things down for, maybe, two days? Then it started again. Meanwhile Chase was acting strangely. Keeping these erratic hours. Drinking more than he used to, glued to his computer. I thought that maybe he'd been fired and was looking for something before I could notice but then I saw his search history. Looking back, it all makes sense.

MARISSA
DEVIN'S CHILDHOOD BEST FRIEND

After the air-dancer ate Johnny Maybrook, we followed it back to Ridonkulous Rick's. Just to be sure that it didn't make detours, decide to snack on someone else. Midway it stopped at a pond in the woods to clean Johnny's blood off its face like a cat.

SHERIFF VAUGHN
CHIEF INVESTIGATING OFFICER

When the DNA lab work came back from the city, none of us were that surprised. Mixed in with each of the victim's remains was some of the Devin kid, match after match. We showed what we found to the county DA and started to gear up to make the arrest.

MARISSA
DEVIN'S CHILDHOOD BEST FRIEND

Still don't fully get how they came back to Devin. They weren't, like, transparent about it exactly. DNA evidence? Okay, okay, I guess I'll take your word for that, but what kind of DNA evidence was it? Devin's blood? His spunk or something? My theory is when Devin touched it, that air-dancer right in the dark of its mouth, some part of him entered it, mixed with its essence. Then after that, it killed those boys.

THE CASE OF THE AIR DANCER

MARTIN STEENBERGEN
VICTIM

The next night I knew it was coming for me. I wasn't about to sit there waiting. So like I'm in some Freddy flick, I armored up. Long pants, long sleeves. Shin protectors, lacrosse mask. Mad-ass duct tape. Came strapped with a baseball bat, weed-whack machete, some ninja stars I bought online, and I took my ass straight to Ridonkulous Rick's. But when I rolled up there, I wasn't as brave. This freezing wind blowing trash over the street. No one else around for miles. And there it was, the air dancer, getting down nasty up there on its mount with that awful face on it that never stops smiling and I started to think of the way it would feel to have that mouth open and take me inside. Would it have teeth to rip and tear or a long purple tunnel of sweaty-ass nylon? And almost like it heard me thinking, it started to do this crazy sway, not side to side but in a circle, almost like it was trying to launch itself off and then I hear, "Hey, Steenbergen! What the hell are you doing out here by yourself?" Marissa and the Devin kid. They were standing behind me. They wanted to dance.

MARISSA
DEVIN'S CHILDHOOD BEST FRIEND

Oh. My. God. You should've seen him, like an extra from some *Mad Max* movie. When I called, "Martin!" Martin turned and that's when the air-dancer, like, came to life, blowing up straight with its arms straight along before starting to claw its way off of its mount. The way that it did that: arms hooked in the ground, wedged down in the sidewalk seam, almost like claws. It clawed itself forward and shucked itself loose. We heard this sound, sort of like Velcro unsticking. Martin saw our eyes get wide and saw the thing coming and screamed like a girl. Dropped his yard-machete thing. The air-dancer was already stretching its mouth when Devin ran past me and Martin right at it. And then he stopped and stared it down. I kid you not, like, nose to nose with the air-dancer crouching on those little arms and Devin in front of it, hands at his sides. It looked like they were going to wrestle. But Devin did the weirdest thing. He patted the air-dancer, once, on its face. Between its eyes, like testing, once. And then Devin started to pet and to stroke it. And like some huge, deformed-ass cat, the air-dancer leaned into Devin's caresses. Nuzzling into his hand, sort of stretching. Soon Devin was down on his knees alongside it with his arms wrapped around its impossible neck. Crooning to it, saying, "Shhhhhhh. You don't need to kill anymore. It's okay." And then we heard a sound behind us, the rattling of a chain-link fence. We all turned around to see who or what made it. "What are you doing here, Dad?" Devin said.

SHERIFF VAUGHN
CHIEF INVESTIGATING OFFICER

Wasn't so long after that Devin's dad turned himself in for the murders. Seemed a little fishy, sure, as when Logan died he had been out of town, but to all of our minds the guy's story held up. Said he strangled the boys, one by one, in one place, then moved their bodies to another. To be more specific, his buddy Ross Quint's: tomato farm just off the highway. Got a pretty six acres. Irrigation works, tractors. And, yeah, that's right, a log-chipper. That's how he said he ground the bodies—unbeknownst to Quint, of course. Said he did it between six and eight in the morning, when the semi's are loudest out there on the road and then at night he strolled through town, depositing bits of them down in the gutters. [commentary off-camera] A little far-fetched, but the crime-scene forensics stacked up like he told them. And besides, we were ready to have it all over. The whole damn town was going nuts! He said that he'd done what he did to those boys because of what they'd done to Devin. Booked him, tried him. Guy got life. He's in there now and there he'll stay.

LEILA
DEVIN'S MOM

I get so mad at Chase sometimes, but was there any other way? If it hadn't been Chase then it would've been Devin. In prison, he wouldn't have made it past lunch. And I think, in his way, Chase did it *for* Devin, to make up for all that he'd missed as a Dad. And I don't mean just plays and birthdays, but missed as in just never noticed. Devin parading past Chase all these years, not so much needing his attention but just to show Chase that he was who he was, and Chase would look the other way. Not because he was ashamed. Because Chase didn't know how to really deal with it or how to love a child like that, even though it was easy. It could've been easy, if only Chase had let it be. So in some way I think that Chase going to prison was him finally saying to Devin—[shields face] Gosh, I didn't expect to get this way! [question off-camera] No, I can keep going. [points at eye and points at camera] It was Chase finally telling him, Now. Now I see.

JACQUI ORVIS
LOGAN ORVIS' MOTHER

I believe he done it, sure. The son of a bitch deserved worse, but I'll take it.

SHERIFF VAUGHN
CHIEF INVESTIGATING OFFICER

Trust me, I've heard all the theories and then some. Devin did it. Devin's dad. This kooky-dook air-dancer theory. But, look: we live on planet earth. The dead stay dead and pigs don't fly. Ridonkulous Rick got the help that he needed. Martin Steenbergen still lives here, drug problems. The girl, Marissa, went to college, now I think works in TV. Devin's dad is still in prison and Devin's mom stayed here in town to be near him. Devin moved off to the city years back. Still lives there, some kind of assumed name or something. Maybe it doesn't add up on the surface but those are the facts of the case, as of now.

MARISSA
DEVIN'S CHILDHOOD BEST FRIEND

Unsurprisingly, maybe, me and Devin lost touch. It's hard to stay friends after something like that. Two years ago, I saw him once. Or, sorry: *her.* I keep forgetting! It's easy to forget sometimes because when I knew her she still was a him and now, you know—I'll just shut up. Got sent to the city to scout some locations. No reason for me not to see her, I guess, so I found her on Facebook but now she's—Devorah! She'd grown her hair out, streaked and layered. Smiling in this summer dress. Cute shade of lipstick, she looked really good. It said "In A Relationship" under her status. Friend-requested her first because why wouldn't I? It was long enough now that the past shouldn't matter and I started to write in the messaging app, "Hey Devorah! How's it going? Been a little while—" But then. [question off-camera] I couldn't keep writing. Whatever upbeat, happy shit I would've written was a lie. The only thing I really felt—like really down deep in myself—was this terror. And I couldn't lie. Not to her. After that. Deleted my words one by one, closed the app. To his day, she hasn't confirmed my request.

RIDONKULOUS RICK
OWNER OF RIDONKULOUS RICK'S AUTOS

Renewed all the bonds that I'd broken, cleaned up. Now I'm back at the dealership moving that metal and the last time I checked we ain't doing half bad. [question off-camera] Uh-huh, still there. Same one as before, too, them shits are expensive! When I'm here late at night, which I try not to be, you bet it creeps me out a little. But then I remember it's just an air-dancer. All it does is sell used cars. In fact, look up and you can see it. Wait for it, wait for it, wait. There it is.

LONG PIG

When Spence goes to open the petting zoo's doors on what he assumes is its last day in business, he discovers MacFarquhar, the petting zoo keeper, lying in blood with his ring finger missing.

Spence gets close. Inspects the wound. The finger has been gnawed away.

The pigs and sheep and goats Spence owns that aren't quite pigs and sheep and goats are mounded in their separate pens.

MacFarquhar's been drinking. That's why he's asleep. He reeks of serf-moonshine, B.O. underneath it. He's half-tipped over on his bench that faces the pens where the E-Tures bed down, his arm splayed out across the bench. The arm is splayed in such a way its wrist and fingers twist up slightly in the brisk attitude of a concert conductor.

The finger shows a ridge of bone. Bloods pumps from the hollow encasing the joint.

"MacFarquhar, MacFarquhar," Spence says, drawing closer.

Spence doesn't need to address him by name, but still he does it out of habit. MacFarquhar has one, after all. The fed listed it on the DSAT (Department of Serf Acquisition and Tenure) when Spence had logged on to select him.

Spence should elevate the hand, but it already is more or less. So he leaves it.

Next Spence goes to check the E-Tures, who never fail to sour his mood, reminders as they are to Spence of the failed enterprise over which he is sovereign and by extension all mankind: the petting zoo, open for nearly a decade.

The petting zoo, once inundated by seekers.

The petting zoo, now: un-trafficked, insolvent.

He'd first put up money to open the place from returns on investments he'd made in the first several months of the Great Cross-Extinction and, where it was needed, the extra he'd saved to one day send Emmie, his daughter, to college. Most of Spence's investments had been in biotech, which was the industry responsible for creating the E-Tures. So thanks to Spence and others like him, gazing onto far horizons, when the last several species turned up as endangered, the technology had been long in the works.

The dying took place with no set hierarchy, though most people thought it had started with livestock, worked its way across from there. Reptiles, rodents. Insects. Birds. Felines and canines of all shapes and types. By the time it had spread to the largest land mammals and begun to show up in the ones in the sea, Spence had stopped watching the news coverage of it.

Now Spence stands before the pens, two prods in his right hand and one in his left. Each genus of E-Ture requires its own prod, coded to its nervous system.

The blood pools and drips from the zookeeper's bench, but none of the E-Tures appear to need prodding. Asleep isn't how Spence would put it. In sleep mode? The E-Tures do need to be charged, after all. There's a USB cord running in through their rectums, connected to the charging hub, the hub itself a black rectangle with a blue power cylinder sheathed in its middle, sitting in the charging bay between Spence's office and where the pens sit, which is MacFarquhar's living quarters—a courtyard covered by a tarp.

MacFarquhar's bench defines this space, sweatpants-inside-sweatpants bunched up for a pillow. Everything else—MacFarquhar's dishes, MacFarquhar's books and magazines, a jar of whatever MacFarquhar's been drinking—must fit beneath the bench and does.

Spence moves among the E-Ture pens, looking for MacFarquhar's finger, but the digit is nowhere in any of them. Can the E-Tures have eaten it up altogether?

All that belies them as lawn ornaments is a faint humming sound at the centers of them. The pigs' snouts are faintly wet, their mouths arranged in secret smiles. The goats with their little legs curdled beneath them.

Spence returns to MacFarquhar, beginning to stir. "MacFarquhar," Spence whispers again with annoyance. Then he nudges Macfarquhar's left flank with his knee.

"Right!" MacFarquhar says, "I'm up."

"What happened?" says Spence.

"Holy hell," says MacFarquar. He unkinks his body and slowly arises. His discomfort appears to have gone to his head, which he rubs with the wince of the badly hung-over. "One of the goats," MacFarquhar says. "Got me when I wasn't looking."

Of course this would happen today of all days with so much to do before closing the zoo. With so many closing promotions at stake and one ceremony to mark the occasion: a glossy banner to be hung, a three-for-one charge on unlimited petting, a "Westminster E-Ture Show" (Spence's concept) complete with a grand promenade and prize ribbons, as well as a speech he'd been writing for days he'll deliver that night on the petting zoo's steps with all of the E-Tures assembled below him. In it, Spence will speak of "hope," the "grit to fight another day."

Emmie, his daughter, has promised she'll be there. Or anyway Emmie's mom, Kay, promised Spence, who divorced him around when he started the zoo, the Great Cross-Extinction in full swing by then. The divorce's intense acrimony aside, her timing had always struck Spence as unkind.

Today is the first day in quite a long time that Emmie will come visit Spence at the zoo. So Spence must admit that he's nervous today. MacFarquhar's finger isn't helping.

Spence examines MacFarquhar still rubbing his head while trying to cut off blood flow to his hand, a tricky balance to achieve. That's when it comes to him MacFarquhar passed out probably not from the moonshine he drank but the pain. Or maybe from some combination. "How did he get out?" asks Spence.

"He didn't," MacFarquhar says, "this was at dinner."

"Dinner?" says Spence.

"While I had them plugged in. That one there." MacFarquhar points to one of the goats, which could be any of them, except for the fact it's the only one standing. It stands toward the back of the pen, its head raised. Spence can see its eyes shining at brief intervals when it twitches its head as though listening for something.

"How long's it been like that?" says Spence.

"Few hours now," MacFarquhar says. "How long I been sleeping?"

But Spence doesn't answer. "After it bit off your finger, what happened?"

MacFarquhar shrugs, grimaces. "Oh, not a lot. I rounded them up, put them back in their pens. That's when I started getting drunk."

Spence pauses a moment, intent on MacFarquhar. That

MacFarquhar decided to finish his chores isn't what surprises Spence. What does surprise Spence—what impresses him, even— is that he was able to do it at all.

"Something wrong?" says MacFarquhar.

Spence smiles. "Not at all. Let's get you bandaged up."

After tending MacFarquhar, Spence puts up the banner.

He posts the unlimited petting promotion. He sets up the "Westminster E-Ture Show" run and arranges the ribbons inside a vitrine. Standing before the bathroom mirror, he even rehearses his speech several times, but is shocked by how little conviction is in it. The parts of the speech that at first had so moved him, peppered with words like "hope" and "moxie," die off in his earholes as patently false. So he tries to recite it as though to his daughter—Emmie, eleven, no, twelve by that point. As though where he sees himself, Emmie is standing, in the sweater she wears with the ears on the hood and the claws on the sleeves that Spence finds so off-putting, because it reminds him of what's dead and gone.

MacFarquhar helps Spence with the zoo preparations, wincing under his hand and his raging hangover. Spence must say the bandage job he did on the zookeeper's hand is half-decent, what remains of the joint stabilized with a splint and only a few spots of blood showing through. Before he'd wrapped and tucked the bandage, Spence had even attempted to trim back the skin that the jaws of the E-Ture had left hanging ragged. MacFarquhar's breathing barely quickened. The man is much tougher than Spence had imagined.

But so are the E-Tures, which makes Spence uneasy. Colder,

more brutal, like actual creatures. Spence tries to think back if he's heard of more cases of E-Tures attacking a live human being and can't think of any outright, though there must be.

The E-Ture simulacrum is purportedly exact, right down to the muscles, the teeth and the hooves. Only the E-Tures' brains are synthetic, and part of the spine, threading into the flesh. The rest of the body—the blood, fat and tissue—is a fully regenerative cellular casing stimulated by signals that come from the brain. These signals are electrical, hence the E-Tures' trademark name. And hence, too, the barely discernible humming that so many mistake for breath.

The trickle of seekers starts early that day. Slightly more of them than normal.

Spence calls them seekers because they are seeking some vestige of the world they knew, a world that had used to have many things in it apart from high primates deserted by luck. Most of the seekers are, tellingly, children, and today they come into the zoo in short bursts: shrieking, writhing, holding hands with siblings or schoolmates or one/both parents, veering here and charging there, pointing at everything, tugging each other, slightly damp from the rain that is falling outside, their hair tangled, their glasses fogged.

MacFarquhar hangs back at the edges of things.

Just left of the door, in his zookeeper's suit, cradling his bandaged hand, he watches the children go into the zoo, pay their fares at the booth and go on to the pens. Spence has never quite trusted MacFarfquhar with children, though nothing he's done has been cause for concern. It's more just a feeling Spence gets—an unwellness. MacFarquhar's eyes a bit too steady as he watches the children make off toward the pens. MacFarquhar's smile a bit too sweet as he outfits the children with paddling brushes so they won't pick up crud from the E-Tures' fur.

Spence never chose MacFarquhar as his serf. MacFarquhar was assigned to Spence after the Great Cross-Extinction was over, his name among the many names of the world's livestock farmers made to pay reparations for supposedly starting the Great Cross-Extinction when a pathogen strain that was masked as a hormone was introduced into the cow population.

Or was it the pigs? Spence can never be sure. No one really is, in fact. The animals were dying off and someone had to take the blame.

Emmie comes through the door not with Kay but with Beaufort, Emmie's stepfather, who Spence doesn't care for. Spence can only assume Kay herself never comes because she can't stand being in Spence's presence so she always sends Beaufort, her lame emissary, to yuck it up and bond with Spence while keeping an eye, very subtly, on Emmie.

The petting zoo's a single room: admission booth just past the entrance, the three E-Ture pens, separated by species, organized beyond the booth. Emmie and Beaufort walk straight up to Spence, who's running cards and making change before giving people their tickets to enter. He starts to come around to Emmie but something displeased in her eyes warns him off, so he awkwardly pivots back where he was standing, reaches down to fluff her hair. "Hey there, sweetheart," Spence says.

"Hi, Dad," Emmie answers. Beneath her bangs her eyes flash up.

"How goes it, Doctor Spence?" says Beaufort, indulging an unfunny habit he has of calling Spence "Doctor" because of the zoo, like Spence must need a PhD to care for robot pigs and goats. "I wish this were all under better conditions but you had a good run of it, didn't you, Doc?"

Spence turns to his daughter, hands shoved in her hoodie. "So, what," says Spence and cuffs her lightly. "You want to go see Mr. Oinks-a-lot first?"

Mr. Oinks-a-lot is Emmie's favorite, the biggest E-Ture in the zoo. When Emmie had come to the zoo in years past, she would always go pet Mr. Oinks-a-lot first, cooing over his rump with her paddle brush, whispering. "Mr. Oinks-a-lot's gross," Emmie says. "He's a monster."

Spence feels his face twisting into a scowl. "That's suddenly an issue for you?"

Emmie rolls her eyes at Spence and turns to look around the zoo.

Beaufort kneels before Emmie and flicks at her bangs. "Hey, monsters can be cool," he says. "Aren't I a cool monster?" Beaufort pulls a face. "How about now?" He pulls another.

"You're such a dork, Beaufort," Emmie says, but even Spence can see she's smiling.

Spence follows Beaufort and Emmie along toward the pens where the children commune with the E-Tures. He swears he can feel the damp eyes of MacFarquhar tracking them across the floor but when Spence looks back at his serf, he's off, walking. Demonstratively busy completing some task.

When they get to the pens Emmie stops and stands slouched. She seems so blasé, so resistant to joy. That can't be healthy for her, can it? Chalk it up to Kay's influence.

He's so sidetracked observing her he almost doesn't see the children. They're closing in a narrow skirt around the goat-pen, whispering. Awed.

Spence isn't sure of the moment in time the petting zoo began to fail. It may not have been a particular moment but rather a long and depressing accretion—the crowds going from loud and spilling to suddenly smaller but no cause for panic, to abysmal and echoing late in year eight when Spence started noticing revenue problems. At first, he didn't quite know why. His E-Tures were top-of-the-line in the biz. He ran the place clean. He charged sober admission. When one day he noticed a father and daughter of roughly his and Emmie's age standing in front of the sheep pen, despondent. Their heads tilted, their faces slack. "It's not really the same, is it, sweetie?" said the father. The daughter frowned and shook her head.

Not a week after that, Spence had finally relented, ordering MacFarquhar from the DSAT. He'd always resisted the notion of serfdom—on moral/ethical grounds, okay, sure, but also in terms of his own self-sufficiency. He'd never needed anyone to help him run the petting zoo. At least MacFarquhar, in his serfdom, had never cost more than it took to feed him, heat his quarters, change his bench-clothes.

Spence pulls his daughter through the kids, her stepdad Beaufort close behind them. There's something magic going on, the children's movements slow, deliberate, like whatever it is they're thronging toward might vanish if they go too fast.

In front of the crowd is the very same goat that took MacFarquhar's finger from him. And the goat is resplendent. Its coat shines in glory. Its musculature is a study in contour. Its eyes spark with this greenish orange, its slotted pupils glossy black. Even how it stands there is more lithe, more alive: its forelegs tensed, its rump perked faintly.

"She's a pretty one, huh?" Beaufort comments to Emmie, but Emmie isn't looking at him.

She's looking at Spence with this light in her eyes. "I love him," she says to her father. "I love him!"

Counting the box at the end of the day, Spence finds that the zoo has done such ample business he could, if he wanted to, open tomorrow, maybe into the start of the following week.

"How's the hand?" Spence asks MacFarquhar.

At the end of MacFarquhar's bed/bench, Spence sits down.

The petting zoo is closed for now. The bathrooms cleaned, the pastures swept. MacFarquhar is resting, his head on the sweatpants, his hand elevated on top of his chest.

"I'll be honest," says MacFarquhar, "a lot better with all five fingers."

"Probably time to change that dressing." Spence sets a first aid kid on top of the bench. "Here," he says, leans in. "Let me."

Slowly, Spence unwraps the bandage, watching MacFarquhar for signs of distress. The angry stump has started crusting, the bone of it mottled partway under scab. Spence judges he did a good job with the scissors: the skin around the wound is clean. When Spence is done coating his serf's hand with ointment and cocooning the hand to the wrist in fresh gauze, he sees that MacFarquhar is gritting his teeth. "You look like you could use a drink."

MacFarquhar surveys him a moment in silence. "I got my own," MarFarquhar says.

He brings up a jam jar from under the bench and starts to unscrew it, but Spence waves him off. "Not that I can say too much after how you hurt your hand, but isn't that moonshine a no-no?" says Spence.

"Sorry, *jefe*," says MacFarquhar.

"Can I ask where you got it?" Spence says.

"Down the way."

"From Perkins or Standish?" Spence says.

MacFarquhar only grins at Spence. Perkins and Standish are neighboring serfs, indentured to people within walking distance, but the serfs are tight-lipped in regards to their business, their clandestine networks, their little rebellions.

"Never mind." Spence pats MacFarquhar's knee. "Got something better. You sit tight."

When he returns moments later with a bottle of scotch, MacFarquhar is sitting erect on the bench. Beyond the bench the sleeping pens, where the E-Tures lie charged and corralled for the night. Or all of the E-Tures except for the goat, who stands alone of all its kind. Infused with a strange and directionless vigor that will not let it rest its head. Eyes shining faintly in the dim, its head cocked to the slightest sound.

By the time Spence is fully attuned to its presence, he sees that MacFarquhar has been for some time. One of his eyes never moves from the goat, its pupil huge and dark with dread.

Spence pours them each a few fingers of scotch. MacFarquhar gulps his down; Spence sips. Spence tilts the bottle at MacFarquhar, and MacFarquhar nods gingerly at him. "Thanks, *jefe*."

Spence pours him more fingers this time and sits back. "Where we you before you came here?"

"With a family."

"They treat you well?"

MacFarquhar shrugs. "Didn't work me too hard, so I guess so," he says.

"How about before that?"

"In a warehouse," he says.

Spence sips his drink. "I don't mean that. I mean *before* before."

"Pig farm," says MacFarquhar. "I run it myself. We really never talked about it?"

Spence shakes his head at MacFarquhar. "No, sir."

The liquor spills up to the rim of the glass before vanishing into MacFarquhar's dark mouth. "Wow-wee-woo! Now that's the stuff." His eyes have begun to look slightly decentered. He gestures for Spence to please pour him another.

"Ten or so acres," he says, "in the country. Ran a tight little slaughter. Real nice operation."

"What happened?" says Spence.

"You're asking me. One day they up and took it from me."

MacFarquhar sips his third glass slower, watching the E-Tures at rest in their pens. He looks contemplative to Spence, possessed of some vital and rarified wisdom.

"So," says Spence, "what do you think?" MacFarquhar slits his eyes, unsure. "You think it was justified—what they did to you? You think the farmers caused all this?"

MacFarquhar's eyes relax; he smiles. "Who cares what I think," he says.

The following day, Spence re-opens the zoo.

At first, he feels foolish unlocking the doors, repurposing the closing banner so it reads "Grand Re-Opening" scrawled on the back, thoroughly cleaning the whole premises, in particular the area between Spence's office and the pens where the E-Tures bed down for the night, but the people start coming by ones and by twos. Then after lunch they come in scores. At 1:15 Spence checks the rolls and counts an intake of well over two hundred. Spence imagines this might be because of the swerve from being closed to being open, the unexpected novelty that arises in the vacuum of something revoked being offered again.

But really Spence knows it's because of the E-Tures: the goat that took MacFarquhar's finger, but also two sheep and the giant prize pig named Mr. Oinks-a-lot by Emmie. Word has spread, Spence assumes, that these E-Tures are different.

And the E-Tures are different, in curious ways.

The goat still has its shimmer-fur, its sculpted contours and its pert way of standing, but these have been joined by a fresh energy, a habit of prancing and sniffing around and a playfulness, even, among the ranked children, who stand at the margins and ruffle its back. As for the sheep, they are creampuffs, meringues; their heads sleek and black, their fur buttered and springy. But Mr. Oinks-a-lot's the prince.

Immense and voluptuous, shifting his bulk, as though daring the seekers to kill and devour him. His crinkly and bursting soufflé of a tummy. His debonair ears, one of them drooping slightly. His little mincing black-tipped legs that present the appearance, when he walks, of infinitesimally hovering forward.

Even Emmie, lukewarm on him just yesterday, appears besotted once again.

Again she arrives at the zoo with her stepdad, leading him on through the doors like a dope. Spence can't remember the last time he's seen her two times in a span of consecutive days, which means that if she's here, again, then coming was her own idea.

Spence watches her as she stands with her stepdad, watching Mr. Oinks-a-lot be fawned over, giggling. Beaufort leans down to make jokes in her ear but Emmie doesn't even hear him, always turning around for her father, for Spence, to grin at him and puff her cheeks in a child's mirroring of the monster before her.

It makes Spence ecstatic. But also uneasy.

Can Mr. Oinks-a-lot be trusted to not harm the children? Harm Emmie? Can any of the E-Tures, in their new dispositions?

Spence decides it will be fine.

After lunch he asks Beaufort to supervise things, hunkers down in his office behind his computer. When the DSAT website has Spence list the reason MacFarquhar's indenture did not "come to term" from a drop-down of reasons prescribed by the site that range from "Displayed antisocial behavior" to "Refused to work" to "Exhibited incompetence," Spence selects it: "Serf absconded."

The confirmation page assures that Spence's case will be reviewed.

For now there's only Emmie, though. She's still with Mr. Oinks-a-lot. A huge group of saucer-eyed children surrounds her. The overripe pig struts in front of the children, its mouth twisted into a brainless half-smile.

Spence comes behind Emmie and seizes her waist. She leans back in her father's arms. He drenches his nose in her hair. It's still there: fruit shampoo with notes of salt.

A recollection comes to Spence, like a jerky quick cut in a film, and then gone: Spence throwing a mop bucket over the floor between his office and the pens, the hot water sluicing over the concrete, pushing out a tide of blood.

"He looks real, daddy," Emmie says. "Is he—" she hesitates "—*can* he be real?"

"No," says Spence. "But let's pretend. Let's pretend that he is for as long as we can."

Mr. Oinks-a-lot reminds Spence of something. What is it?

Long pig: the name for human meat.

Spence peers over Emmie, sees Beaufort beyond, who's smiling rigidly at Spence, his hand balancing on the top of the pigpen. Clownish, sloppy seconds Beaufort, as fake as the E-Tures corralled in their yards.

It's not hard to imagine him slipping, careening. Spence would pull him out, of course. But it's not hard for Spence to imagine it happening, how Emmie would laugh and how Spence would feel bad.

He leaves his daughter, goes to Beaufort. Puts his hand on Beaufort's arm. "Kids," says Spence. "It takes a village."

Beaufort only nods at first, but then he remembers his manners: "Sure, Doc."

Only because he's so pathetic, Spence will have to invite the man over for drinks. It will probably be awkward between them at first, the potential for growing uncivil enormous. But Spence will have to toe the line. He'll have to be the better man.

THE BURIAL PARTY

In her invalid's bunk on the steamer *Virginia*, the Nurse cannot stop throwing up.

When the boat is in motion, it does not afflict her. She could stand on the prow with her face in the wind. But when the steamboat lies at anchor in the hot airlessness of the day, churning faintly, the Nurse's insides fly apart. She becomes, to herself, an intemperate stranger.

In his starched uniform with its loud epaulets, the Quartermaster stands above her. "It is an absurd proposition," he says.

"Absurd," she says, "in what regard?"

The Quartermaster does not help to keep the vomit from her throat. He has come all the way below-decks to berate her for simply being who she is. "It will squander manpower and rations," he says, "in grave excess of what we have. I will telegraph Meigs and inform him, all right?"

He means the Quartermaster General. She lurches for her pail of sick and coughs up burning yellow strings. "I will carry on with or without..." The Nurse pauses. She fights down the vomit, her hand at her mouth. "The Private will accompany me."

"The Private will accompany you," says the man in her bunk, "to the dock for desertion."

It's summer 1865. They are headed to Andersonville in the south with their rolls of accursed, unaccounted for names: fallen soldiers never found. There is the Nurse, the Quartermaster, the Private, and the many men—forty-odd government workers and craftsmen with seven thousand white headboards that are to be planted at Andersonville for twice as many Union dead. At the prison itself, also known as Camp Sumter, or the Final Depot or the Maw of Fresh Hell, thirteen thousand Union boys have not been buried in their graves. The Georgia Railroad is in shreds from Sherman's blood-march to the sea, though a clerk has mapped for her an alternate route that will take them by riverboat up to Augusta, by rail to Atlanta, then southeast to Macon, at that point only dropping down to enter the prison by points south. Awaiting Meigs' confirmation for the burial party to keep moving forward, the ship has been moored on the Savannah River for nearly a week now. July is in earnest. What is fact and what is fever churn behind the Nurse's eyes. She's seen boys half her age explode into confetti. Red mazes of guts in the plain light of day. But only now over this middling chop do the biscuits and rashers come up in her throat.

With her handkerchief pressed shakily to her mouth, she looks up at the Quartermaster. "When I come above-decks in a moment," she says, "we will discuss this matter more."

"Don't hurry yourself, Madam Nurse." He goes out. She hears him stop along the hall. The Quartermaster says, "Enough." She has heard him discussing her now many times—above-decks, in the diner, outside of her door. He always says the same nine words: "Some people aren't fit to go anywhere, are they?"

She pushes her pail of sick under the bed. She buttons the front of her dress to the collar. The river through her cabin glass resembles a basin of wobbling pus.

The next day Meigs will telegraph for them to "take the round-about" and their own Quartermaster will wallow in gin, stomping wretched and slurred through the ship in the night. At three past midnight, maybe four, the Army Nurse will wake to scratching, prying at her cabin door, yet by the time she understands the person who is there outside, he will have dragged himself away up the steamer's gangplank to collapse on the deck, where come the next day he will find himself sprawled in his dress uniform with a mouth full of rot.

The Quartermaster wakes in pain beneath the shadow of the oaks. The oaks themselves are hulking, dark, entwining in agony over the river. He lies on the poop deck in all of his clothes. Though it is scarcely after dawn, already the air is competing with steam.

"The South," he says. "The cunting South." He says it aloud, torn apart by hangover. He has served at New Orleans, Bull Run, and Antietam.

The Private swivels into view. He's been standing above him, just off to the right. No telling, really, for how long. He stands as he always does, pale, deferential, hoping somebody will give him his orders. The Private was taken at Andersonville for nearly a year before being turned loose when Sherman's armies took Atlanta. His body and face bear the ghoulishness of it—emaciate, wan, always seemingly bruised. The Private is responsible for landing him here on this ship with the Nurse. The Private gave her what she needed—the long roll of names of the lost Union dead—and the Nurse promptly went to the government with it. The Private appeared out of nowhere, it seemed, like a specter from Dickens, with good information.

Yet in truth he reminds him of no one so much as a man he had served with in the 12th of Pennsylvania—an Austrian wisp by the name of Van Cleave. Van Cleave had not been cut for war. He pissed himself at cannonades. And worse, when the dirt-blast came showering down, he crouched and gripped his skull for cover. The unit called him this: Van Quease. The Private is different than Van Quease, however. He's just as skinny, yes, there's that, and seemingly unfit for war, but there's also a dark otherworldliness in him that discomfits the Quartermaster, like the Private has been to the depths of the pit and drunk in its foulness without going blind.

The Quartermaster can't believe that he is here and not back home.

When he drags himself into a leaning position, smacking his mouth with the terrible taste, he finds the sun is in his eyes and he says to the Private, "A bit to the left."

With the faintest delay between hearing and action, the Private's heels snap as he moves to obey him. "Perfect," says the Quartermaster. "Now stay where you are, very still, until lunch."

The Private starts rifling his pockets for something. "You left this on the foredeck, sir."

"I do sincerely hope," he says, "that you are reaching for your flask," but the Private hands over a cameo locket.

About last night, now he is clearer: the Quartermaster has a notion of giving himself to the still, darkened river. Of standing on the foredeck with his hands in the air while cursing the fates that have battered his life. The portrait is a cameo of the woman who once he'd called "fiancé." It opens on a golden hinge. The face is enclosed by a backing of jet. He vaguely remembers the locket

held open, wavering before his face. He had been hoarsely screaming at it, calling it names that are foul to a woman. "Thank you,
Private. Very good."

As the Private backs away from him, the Nurse surfaces above-
deck. She has not been outside her bunk since they first anchored
here at the mouth of the river and she moves with a lumpen, enfee-
bled aspect belying just how young she is. He might've been more
of a gentleman to her had she only admitted when she had been
beat, but her illness had rendered her more of a thorn, increasing
her permanent need to "press on," a phrase that irritates him worse
than anything she might've said, for it means, in his mind, that he
cannot press on. "You are primed for the day, it appears," he says to
her, hiding the locket away in his coat.

Ignoring his words, the Nurse turns to the Private, but she
cannot resist him and whips back around. "You are still in your
cups from last night. It's disgusting."

"How could I *ever* fail to be"—he starts walking backward—"with someone like you?"

Anchor line lies coiled behind him. He stumbles upon it and
catches his balance, one leg hopping underneath him. "Assemble
the men," the Nurse says to the Private.

"Half of them are gone ashore, ma'am."

The Private regards her attentively, waiting. The Quartermaster
would like for the Private to hate her but he seems to regard her
with sheepish affection. Everything she says to him he seems to
hear, *Mind you, change that dressing.*

The Private will go off to do as she says, borne away on his
gangly, cadaverous limbs, walking into Savannah's whorehouses and
taverns like one alien to his own appetites and the men will come
staggering back to the boat in ragged processions of several and

few. The Quartermaster won't see their return; he will hear it, biv-
ouacked below-decks in his room, his head splitting. Mostly, he'll
be occupied never starting completely the same lovelorn letter, his
crumpled attempts, like the Nurse's sick napkins, littering his cabin
floor. He will write: *Dear Lenore...* He will write: *Dearest Len...*
He will write: *Dear Beloved Lenore...* and redact it. The salutation
will take hours. *I realize you think me changed since I was delivered
from war's fiery belly—that I have griefs and fits and fears beyond
what you can understand—but let me assure you, oh light of my life,
my love for you has never changed.* All the way to Augusta, shut up
in his berth, he will not have a single sip, determined to be spic and
span when they dock and debark for the train to Atlanta. Horrors
unreckoned will take him at first. A Sergeant-Major's mustached
face disintegrating under fire, turning into an absence that fronted
a head. Van Quease stirring in his bed, his fear-scarlet eyes coming
groggily open, his lips drawing up from his teeth in alarm when his
cheek first encountered the blood on his pillow. Before the boat can
even dock he will put on his blues with the yellow chevron, make
handsome his whiskers and go up on deck, anxiously seeking out
word of the Private to insist that the thousands of white-washed
headboards be carried ashore in advance of the rest, but he will find
the Private nowhere. He will go knocking at his door in irritated
disbelief and it will be a quarter-hour before the man stands there
in filthy pajamas. The Private will knuckle his eyes in a daze. And
then he will say, "Have we come to the place?

The dead might speak at any time. The Private cannot miss a word.
Shut up in his car on the train to Atlanta, he means to improve

on the way that he listens. He means to block out other sounds save the ambient clack of the train in its motion so when the dead come rising up, he'll be able to parse them from that other sound. In his own private car, he can't hear the men's voices: their alien deepness, the sidle of them. They are principally Negros, now all of them freedmen. For them, he fought a civil war.

A knock comes at the Private's door. He ignores it a moment and hopes it will pass. When the knock comes again, he gets up to see to it if only to have the car silent again and it is the Nurse who stands there in the door, her hair parted evenly down to the scalp. "Accommodations suit you, Private?"

"Most graciously, ma'am."

"May I come in and sit?" She sees the hesitation on his face. "Just a moment."

He opens himself, like a hinge, from the door. While the nurse spreads her skirts to sit down, he stays standing. "Feeling better, ma'am, I take it?"

"I am tolerable, Private."

"That is happy to hear."

"You have seen the cargo we are carrying with us?"

"The wooden plaques, ma'am."

"And you know their appointment?"

"They are to be planted," he says, "for the fallen."

"As many as we can find out. It is to be a cemetery. I dare say, Private," says the Nurse, "there would be no mission were you not here with us."

The Private stares blankly at her; he is listening. He knows, of course, that she is right. To him had the list of dead names been dictated. His hand had inscribed them upon the papyrus. And it had been him who had gone to the nurse, the list tucked tight against his skin. "You have never once mentioned yourself in all this, is all I mean to say," she says. "If you are the locus of some private pain? Some sorrow that remains unsaid. If there is someone's Christian name," she looks up at him, "that requires an inscription."

He thinks the name—*John*—but doesn't say it; it drives like an icicle into his brain, but it can't pass his lips—*January*—not yet. "There are so many names worth remembering, ma'am."

"Which is to say you have no one?"

John January. The Private nods mildly. "I come as a vehicle, ma'am. Nothing more."

"A medium, you mean?" she says.

The Private pauses, wondering. What does she expect him to say? He says, "Yes."

A deep satisfaction comes over her face. She smiles and says, "Well."

Then she gathers herself. The Private is still standing up.

The Nurse goes out the door and it shuttles behind her.

He stands in the car, listening. Then he sits. He sits erect, as he is trained. The car clacks and sways with the curve of the land, and the lantern above him hides things, then reveals them. He hears John January's voice. It tells him: *Go back to the door and look out.*

There's only the dim serpentine of the car. More lantern-light sways from a hook further down. The carpet is a wooly red, the color of blood in a vaudeville play. The train rolls and clacks underfoot. He stands waiting. He strains his ears to hear the voice.

It says: *Do you see me?*

"Not yet."

Here I come.

The door to the subsequent car shuttles open. The Private steps into the hall and stands braced. A skin-colored something begins down the car, moving low to the ground with a dragging and scratching. The top of a head that looks violently bald falls into the lantern light, face to the floor. The hackles of a spine come next. What resolves as a naked and limbless torso is making its way through the gloom toward the Private, propelling itself down the length of the car by convulsing its shoulders and twisting its waist. The arms are sheer. The legs are stumps. The face is turned into the floor.

Between grunting and gasping, it whispers: *How long?*

"A hundred and twenty miles yet," says the Private.

Say the hours.

The Private thinks. "A day and a night and a day, as the crow."

John January groans: *Sooo looong.*

"The way ahead is compromised. We have had to make do with an alternate route."

Compromised?

"Due to the war."

Tell us which.

It is not a question the Private can answer.

John January nears him now. *It weighs on us to wait so long.*

"They will follow your names to the ends of the earth."

They are our names, he says, *no longer.*

He sniffs the Private's leather shoes. With his neck straining up from the blood-colored rug, he turns his face into the light.

The Private does not see him now. He sees him as he was before. He sees him, his cellmate in Andersonville, if a cell it could even be feasibly called—more a stable for fattening cattle or swine with a ripped canvas tent stretching over the top in which upwards of two-dozen men slid about in the blackened, rank mud of their own filth and piss. John January is one of these men. He stares at the

Private through veils of lost time.

At that point, just his right leg had been shot away; he was still sovereign of his left leg and arms. He leaned against the stockade fence, his good foot sunk up to the heel in black mud. He was smoking a cigarette, sacred of objects, having bargained its likeness enough for three more from one of the less hateful guards in the place. He assembled another and passed to the Private. He lit it for him with the end of his own.

"Hold the smoke," he told the Private. "No matter what happens, you can't let it go."

In the train rushing on through the hot Georgia night, John January turns around. It's a weird, semi-crablike maneuver he makes in the narrow confines of the car; it is awful. As his scarred and depleted buttocks move away, the stumps of his legs kicking up as he goes, he whispers to the Private: *Soon.*

The Private stands and watches him until the door opens and swallows him whole and imagines him moving prone over the trestle, insects and grit whipping over his back.

All through the rest of the trip to Atlanta, the Private will not close his eyes. The train will enter, circumspect, through a long corridor of upheaval and wrack—the splintered containers, the wrecked shells of depots, a scorched locomotive tipped onto its side, its cowcatcher scraping the incoming train with tiny expulsions of sparks as it passes. When the train enters what now remains of the station, the Private, Quartermaster, and dozens of workers, supervised by the Nurse, will unload in the heat. In the shade of a crumbling and freestanding wall that had formerly served as a side of the depot, a woman dressed in widow's weeds will rise and begin toward the party of men. Though her bombazine veil and her dress of black silk suggest she is someone of elegant breeding, the Private will see that her face is dirt-smeared, her fingernails chewed to the quick. She will stink. The Private will be close enough to observe of the woman how awful she smells because of the way she approaches the party—dawdling at first in the shade of the wall before picking up terrible, animal speed and rushing the Nurse where she stands giving orders, interposing herself, shouting, "Murderers! Devils!" The Nurse will hold her by the shoulders, raise her palm and slap her, hard. Moaning, the woman will stagger away, the dark of her dress billowing in the sun. On the wagons they charter to carry them south, the Private will sit at the reins of the lead and he will have visions of Andersonville as a crater filled up to the top with hot blood. Again and again he will swivel around to see the land that lies behind, expecting to catch sight of John January going mangled and strange in the wake of the train, but all he will see is the Nurse staring at him, sitting straight as a gravestone against the horizon.

The Nurse has never felt so spry. She feels she is entering into her power.

They passed Macon some time ago, the Private in the lead of them. Then Macon's outskirts fall away on low hills, pine forests, a few cotton fields.

It is the journey's final leg, a tipping into what awaits, and it is fitting in her view that the rumbling of engines of ferries and trains has turned to the groaning of wood and packhorses. The wagons allow them to feel closer to it.

As they come into Anderson, sparsest of towns, she wants to

get down off the seat of her wagon, number four in a train of as many, and run. The Nurse is sure the Quartermaster saw to it she was in the back. The overland journey has seen him grow milder, if milder is not speaking to her at all. He rides the second seat, erect, his chevrons pushing off his shoulders, not swaying along with the wagon beneath him but vibrating stiffly, a soldier of soap. She wants to run past him and tip off his hat.

Past the edge of the town, deeper forest surrounds them. Everything is so quiet. Every birdcall is sudden. The rattle of the wagons' wheels becomes invocation pronounced by the trees.

When they pass from the trees, there is Andersonville. On twenty-six acres of two treeless slopes divided by a narrow creek, there are watchtowers, stockade and medical buildings. Beyond the west edge of the camp, at the top of the slope, are the improvised graves: trenches only several feet where prisoners' bodies were tossed by the hundreds, sticks marking the top of the shoveled-in plots to number the vain and anonymous dead. Now they're just mounds with sticks poking out of them, like a garden of trellises dead at the seed. Above the graveyard, where the hill becomes steeper, human-sized holes have been gouged in the earth. These, the Nurse can only guess, were where the men sheltered in terrible storms and sometimes even died amidst when the dirt grew unstable and caved in around them. She hears their wailing even now. She shudders to think on them, bones in their niches.

The wagon train queues at the camp's northern gate. The Nurse is not sure what it was she expected. It is quieter here than it was in the forest. The grass is grown tall, and the trees provide shade. Kudzu spirals up the towers. The lead wagon halts and the Private dismounts.

A blistering tension comes over the group as the Private walks back down the train toward the Nurse. He is the only man along who has been to the prison and come back to tell it.

When the Private had first come to visit the Nurse with the roster of names of the lost Union dead, she had been sitting in her office in the building they gave her in Gallery Place from which to catalogue the dead and give them each a proper home. Officially, its name was this: the Office of the Missing Soldiers. But only from the many men who cycled in dress uniform through its doors had she heard it referred to as the Dead Letter Office, "where casualties went to recover their mail." This on account of the thousands of letters sent out by the Nurse and her writing assistants in reply to the inquiries they had received from the wives and the siblings and parents in search of their husbands and brothers and sons in the field. How one day a person is walking around and writing you letters, and then they are not.

The Private lingered in her door. He had waited to see her, he'd said, for five hours. He might've waited fifteen more. He had a sheet of names in hand. His eyes had been hollows, his physique depleted. His chest had appeared oddly prominent to her, not from aggregate muscle but punishing hunger, the ribs and the stomach so sere with disuse the chest above appeared to bulge. She had thought that the Private had battle fatigue, what they called "soldier's heart" in the few that sought treatment, and while she was not incorrect, there'd been something about him that made her sit straighter.

Had it been fear? Not fear—a hunger.

She knew it was hunger because it was hers. Turning inside her with great, gusting swoops, the hunger the Private had in him but different, and every time it touched her core, the office she sat in would make the Nurse ache with bitter, old humiliation. The office with its street-side windows, its august leather trappings, its great oaken desk.

Before they had put her in charge of the Office, she'd been "Lady in Charge" of the tent hospitals for the Army of the James under General Butler. And when the Union's glory came, the Nurse had expected to be party to it—to march down the main with her brothers in arms, but the Nurse hadn't marched, she had sat in the office. And she had watched the marchers pass. *They would not let me march, you see,* she had wanted to say to everyone when they looked for her face in the crowd and saw no one. *They would not let me march with them because it would lessen their glory by half. Because I am their better in all but the thing that I have where my legs come apart, and that, too.* It was hunger she felt not because she had failed but because she'd been cheated of what she deserved.

What the Private confessed on that day in her office had been too ghastly to be false. He'd been one of the first men in Andersonville; come the Great Turnaround, one of its last survivors. In between, he'd recorded the names of the dead whatever way he'd had to hand—sometimes with tepid, bartered ink on mattress shucks or canvas shreds, sometimes with blood and excrement, his own and maybe other men's, transcribed upon the union suits that their moldering bodies no longer required. Many, he had memorized by repeating them nights as a charm against death.

Before he had fled from the camp he'd compiled them on a tent-wall so large he could barely transport it, and that's how his brethren had found him again, naked and starving and clutching his banner. "Like something," he'd told her, "from somebody's dream."

"A nightmare more like it," had been her response.

"I done what I aimed to," the Private had said. "What happened before I got loose was the nightmare."

He'd handed her the sheet of names. The writing had been so, so small and so condensed upon the page that at first she had doubted it writing at all—the product of a ruined mind. The names had gone on to the opposite side.

She'd asked the Private, "Is that all?"

The prominent chest had appeared to deflate when the Private's hand disappeared under his shirt and emerged with a volume of loose-leaf, inked parchment. He threw it on the Nurse's desk. The shocking thing wasn't the sound that it made, but the new skinniness of the man who had thrown it, a marionette of cloth and bone.

Now she climbs from her seat and embraces the Private in full view of the other men. "Poor courage," she says.

He is like statuary. Beyond his shoulder, workmen watch, a few of them holding their hats to their hearts. They are all veterans of the great conflagration. They have served with Ohio, Vermont, Massachusetts. One of them, his hair shock-white, his left eye a puckered concave, hums a psalm. The Nurse feels a summons to look on these men with the traumatized Private held close to her chest. "The creek," he says. "It's all dried up."

They alight from the wagons and tour the stockade—the Private and a dozen workers. The Quartermaster stays behind with the rest of the men who seem too tired to follow.

The Private narrates what they see: the spindly watchtowers embedded with marksmen that shot down Yankees mid-escape; the hospital sheds where the prisoners were brought to treat their scurvy and gangrene. Out of these they would rarely if ever emerge, requisitioned as subjects of medical torture at the hands of the cruel and insane Captain Wirz. They tread the banks of Stockade Creek, which cuts through the center of camp from the east. It's a lean tributary of Sweet Water Creek where the water runs mineral-potent and clear within rifle shot of the eastern stockade, while the creek through the camp was a sin against nature—a well and a wash-pot, a sink and a privy. A thin lee of grease, now condensed into blubber, still clings eerily to the edge of the banks.

The Nurse is afraid that her breakfast will leave her. It is all so barbaric, inhuman, and sad. "Were the men's miseries not compounded," she says, "to have drinkable water so near to the fence?"

"It did twist the knife in us some," says the Private. "One—his name I can't recall—had a mind to go digging a well in the yard. A little while he got at something but it smelled sulfur-like and it gave him the runs. Kept digging down past it, not eating or sleeping. Fell over face-first in the hole. He drowned in it."

The Private ambles down the creek, talking back over his shoulder, arms swinging. The excitement she'd felt on approaching the camp sheers away, for a moment, on total despair. At the edge of the creek she stops walking and waits. When the party turns back to see whether she's coming, she exhales and recites a restorative verse, "In these brave ranks I see only the gaps. Thinking of dear ones whom the dumb turf wraps."

The Quartermaster says, "James Lowell. Be succored my immortal soul."

She can see he intends his retort to be funny, but none of the men looking back at her laugh.

There are differing thoughts on where they should pitch camp. The Nurse prefers beside the graves as most of their time will be spent digging in them, not to mention the fact should it happen to storm they won't be in the water's way. The Quartermaster, as he's wont, will have no part in her illogic. Major General Stoneman's ill-fated campaign to liberate Andersonville had failed thusly—or so the Quartermaster says. They had come from the east, where the graves are dug in, to encircle the camp and been routed by Rebs. Watching him flounder and choke in the past, the Nurse feels pity for the man for the first time, she's sure, since their party embarked. "If I may, Colonel," says the Nurse, "your service to the cause withstanding, we have not come here on campaign. We have come to fulfill our appointment as men."

"*Some* of us have come for that." Beneath her gaze, the Quartermaster seems poised to say more things that he will regret, but all that comes is, "Have your camp."

He flings his wrist and strides away. She watches him reach some indefinite point in the overgrown field at the center of camp before he stops to curse aloud. Then he turns around again.

As the men set up tents and a wilderness kitchen, the Nurse spurs herself to take matters in hand. She goes to the wagon to seek out the rolls the Private brought her in her office. Then apart from the men, in the lead wagon's shade, she begins to page through them by name and by date, seeing if she can establish a pattern between the death-date and the lay of the graves. Although there had been little hope of finding out which soldier lay in what grave— their bodies by now would be long depreciated by seasons of rainfall, the dank of the earth—the Nurse had insisted to Meigs that they try. When she reaches the last of the names on the rolls, the Nurse starts over once again.

It is only past noon and the southern sun bakes.

The Private does not help the men. The Nurse watches him wandering over the hills like a scout or a sleepwalker, hand at his brow. He seems fixated on the holes that dot the hillside leading up from the graves, as though they emanate a pitch that he of all the men can hear.

When the men are done working, they gather around her. Their camp is positioned just right of the plots with their hundreds of sticks to mark the dead, the holes in the hillside continuing up like the blasphemous tunnels of giant-sized ants. She says, "Gentlemen, there is still daylight left. If there was a time to start digging, it's now."

The workmen grumble, then begin. Their shovels eat into the dirt of the plots.

In half-an-hour's time she will hear her name called by someone or other involved in the digging. Bemused, she will walk to the lip of the hole that the party has dug rapidly in the earth to find several men looking up from the bottom, shifting around with their palms in the air. "Madame Nurse," one will say to her, "ain't nothing here but mud and roots." The Nurse will tell this man dig more. At the height of the work, there will be seven holes, none of them with corpses in them. The Quartermaster will start laughing. And he will laugh so hard and long that he will have to flee the site, rushing into the calm of his officer's tent and rifling his soldier's kit to find two flasks of brandy beneath ammunition. Both of these he will extract.

Before going out to address the campaign, the Quartermaster has a drink.

He empties his boot-flask in three scalding swallows and liquor is a gorgeous thing. It jettisons down from his throat to his chest and radiates out to his hands and his feet. Then he goes out to the site of the graves and hits the Private in the face.

The Private doesn't even flinch, just receives and absorbs his superior's blow. He is still—save a trickle of blood from his mouth.

The Quartermaster hears himself as though from very far away.

"This man is a spy! Do you see?" he announces. "He brings us here on false pretense—to ferret out corpses that cannot be found. He fraternizes—"

"Colonel, please! You are making a terrible scene," says the Nurse. She whispers to him, "Carry on, and the men will lose every last shred of respect. This man," the Nurse continues calmly and louder now so all can hear, "was a prisoner at Andersonville, where you stand. It is a documented fact. He assembled his roster of fallen in secret. He wrote down their names even as they were murdered and dug beneath the dirt like dogs."

The Quartermaster scarcely hears. A likeness clamors in his mind, begging to be understood: if now on the hill with his knuckles skinned open from hitting the Private in front of the men is close to that time in his fiancé's parlor when she had thrown her teacup at him and he had grabbed her by the throat and slammed her up against the wall.

He leaves the site of his disgrace. Down the hill, past the gates, through the field to the trees. His leg that got nicked in a charge at New Orleans, something off with the tendon, no cause for concern, wobbles out at the knee as he crosses the field. He hammers his mouth with the new brandy flask. The forest envelopes him, fragrant and hushed.

At Antietam his cot had lain next to Van Quease's. In the several days after the battle was over as they gathered their kit and recorded the fallen, outside of the tent had been hell on this earth: hogs rooted around in the chests of the dead; crows plucked eyeballs out of skulls. His cowardliness under fire notwithstanding, Van Quease slept best of all the unit. Each morning like clockwork the man would roll over, an expression of deep-seated calm on his face. His eyes still closed in sleep, mouth smacking.

One night when the Quartermaster couldn't sleep he wandered out among the dead. He picked up a head mutilated in skirmish and carried it back through the flap of the tent.

The tangled hair, the staring eyes. The scrim of gore below the neck.

This he set sideways on Van Quease's pillow, left cheek facing down like a lover at rest. Van Quease woke up screaming and sprinted through camp. A sharpshooter woke with his rifle pre-loaded. In the wake of the gunshot the field was so silent, but what he heard was even worse: the sound of his cruel and maniacal laughter echoing among the dead.

The Quartermaster can't go on. He falls to his knees with a wretched, choked sound, puts his hand underneath him and slumps on his rear. He leans against a nearby tree. It's an ancient red hickory, thick in the bark. He follows where it stretches, up, beyond the unwholesome morass of this world, its delicate leaves throwing sunlight above him. He reaches back, claws at the stump. The crusty damp bark comes away in his hand. Then without knowing why and yet knowing precisely, with a bitter surrender that floods through his chest, he shoves the bark inside his mouth and chews it until he can swallow it down. The taste is loamy, almost sweet. Rough shards of tree-bark lodge deep in his throat.

The Quartermaster will remain with his back to the tree until the brandy flask is empty. He will shout at the godhead, "You bastard, make more! You have struck down a half-million men, make more brandy!" The height of his delirium will bring about in him malevolent visions: the dark and robust silhouette of a man who stands on a hill with his back to the trees. In the last of the twilight the figure will turn and he will observe it is Private Van Quease with a sheer prominence where there should be a head—the head itself dangling hair-first from the hand, on the face an expression of sainted contentment. Midway through the night he'll awake to an owl. He'll find that he is still quite drunk. In a fog he will stagger the way that he came, through the trees and the field, past the gate, up the hill, but the ruin that brought him to this point in time will not travel backward, will carry him on. Coming into the camp, which is quiet and still, the Quartermaster will see something: at the top of the gravesite, a wavering flame.

The Private hears the call: *Wake up.*

He hangs in the dark on one elbow. He's listening.

The bodies of a dozen workmen grumble, snore and sigh around him. A lantern sits outside each tent to light the men's ways to the privy at night and by its muffled glow he catches movement in the canvas, a spherical pressure. A whisper, a groan.

Wake up, the voice says. *It is time to come see.*

The Private reaches out his hand and the shape nuzzles in it, a strange, canine warmth. He is wearing a union suit, cover enough. He unbuttons the flap of the tent and goes out.

Already the torso is moving away, past the graves, up the hill, toward the caves on the ridge. With his shoulders propelling him, beating uphill, and the nubs of his legs serving him as a rudder, John January moves over the wash. The Private is no longer horrified by him—the way he is mangled, the way that he moves. There is an eerie elegance to the commonsense way he has seen to evolve.

It awaits you, he calls to the Private, *within.*

He means the caves that dot the hill. They look tailor-made for more John Januarys: the width of his shoulders, the height of his neck. Below him, the Private begins up the incline, sees that John January, above him, has balls. They are rather big balls and they're covered in dirt as he drags them like soldier's kit over the hillside. Soon he's poised at the entrance to one of the caves, his head wrenched around, looking back at the Private. It's a look of profound and unspeakable blankness. He never ever takes it off. And he wears it tonight at the mouth of the cave as he wore it at daybreak in Andersonville in a hole that the Private and him had clawed out for a clean patch of dirt at the edge of the fence—in fact, an operating theater. Because John January had gangrene all over, his arms and the leg he had left would be lost. When the Private began on the reeking black leg with a pocketknife bartered from one of the guards not blood but a clear, sludgy serum leaked out, pooling in ribbons on top of the dirt.

John January tells him, *Come.* He screws himself into the hill and is gone.

The Private rams the dirt face first and makes a little headway in. He corkscrews his torso, breaks through. He is stuck. He tries to wriggle out again. He can still see the leg-stumps of John January paddling through the gloom a few meters ahead where the tunnel appears to be widening, so he gives it his all, clawing further inside. The tendrils of roots bend back over his face, and the dirt showers down in his hair and around him. He hears the whispering again. Not the sphinxlike pronouncements his friend has been making, but something specific—familiar even. John January is chanting the names.

Levi Warren, Horace James, Henry Trumbull, Chauncey Thomas, Henry Turner, Edmund Tuttle, Gamaliel Collins, Oliver Light—

He's saying them now as he said them before through the walls of the rooming house, yellow and thin, where the Private had sheltered in view of the White House in a district they called Murder Bay. The Private had only lived there for a month when the voice of the dead man had come to live with him—in the walls of his room, like a sentient rat. Every name that was told him the Private recorded, and these he had alphabetized for the Nurse. He had known he must go to the Nurse with the names because the voice had told him to, yet the Private had never once questioned the reason, for he is a soldier. Was then and remains.

He is hearing the names in that way once again when suddenly the passage dips. For a moment the Private feels poised, fraught for balance. His stomach pressed in and his torso seesawing. He slams his hands against the dirt. For now, they seem to hold him up. He strains his eyes to see the drop but all he can feel is dark air, blowing upwards.

The Private will go without hindrance or knowing—one direction, down and down. His passage through darkness will end on more stone, an immense chamber of it, enshrined in the hill. He will exit the shaft in a crablike maneuver, skidding forward on his ass, and will think that he sees by a nimbus of torchlight a field of stalagmites that stretches for miles. Meanwhile up above in the land of the living, the Nurse will start climbing the hill in his wake.

The Nurse has brought a lantern with her. She is glad for the way that it swings from her wrist; she feels swaddled up by the light that it casts, maybe four feet in front of her, two on the side.

It was by lantern-light that she first saw the Private and by lantern-light she now keeps him in sight, tracking his path up the side of the hill. When she reaches the cave at the top of the hill where the Private in only his long johns has vanished, she moves it about the interior space: its crumbling walls, its tangled roots. Her flesh recoils instinctively.

But then she remembers her debt to the men, her avowal to Meigs at his government desk, her reassurance to the Private, her terrible, beautiful Seventh Street office. She shrugs the lantern down her arm and ducks her head inside the hole.

Narrow-going but not quite as bad as it looks. She moves on her elbows, the lantern before her. When the shaft interrupts the way forward, she shouts.

She gathers her limbs up, as though from a slag-pit. It's not a place for human beings. But still she sees it's possible with the lantern held carefully over her stomach to voyage downward on her back, which is to say nothing of how she'll return. When she reaches the stone at the base of the shaft, her breath is rasping in her throat.

Her first impression is of volume. As best she can tell, there are fifty-foot ceilings and rows of stalagmites that go on for yards. She takes a step forward. The dark takes a step.

The room is enormous, a vast echo chamber.

She brushes the skin of the rock as she goes. The formations are sparse at the base of the slide but farther on into the chamber they thicken, a gleaming, dark forest of runts and colossi, of crook-ed-backed dancers, of hump-conjoined twins. One moment she's walking, the lantern held high among the stalagmites that cover the floor, and the next one she isn't, the layout has changed. What she thought were stalagmites aren't really at all. Now some of them are separating, doubling before her eyes.

There are figures before her. They watch her advance.

The Nurse looks behind her. More figures are watching.

They wear cloth patchwork masks that are tight on their skulls, the bottoms tucked down into uniform collars. At the base of each mask there's a hole for the mouth.

Behold: their grim and wrinkled lips.

She wraps her hands over the glass of the lantern to feel for a moment the flame's searing heat.

They wear the colors of their armies: blue or grey or patchwork brown. The uniforms are depredated; frayed and scorched, blood-stained and torn. The patchwork masks the figures wear are cobbled up from battle flags: the Confederate cross or the Federal stripes. She almost doesn't see the Private.

Like the figures, he stands near a crop of stalagmites—utterly motionless, utterly silent. She has to double back at first to see the single naked face: the eyes fixed open glassily, the wet, healthy mouth in an idiot's grin. He stands in his underwear, riddled with dirt-stains.

A figure in a chaplain's sash stands next to the Private, uncomfortably close. He is a tent-pole of a man, gaunt and near on seven feet. One bar of the Rebel flag covers his face. A white, bushy beard pushes out of the hole.

"Private, are you there?" she says. "Private, can you hear my voice?"

The Private does not answer her, so she squeezes his arm at the crease of his elbow.

"You are not well." She takes his hand. "Shall I escort you back outside?"

The Chaplain leans down like a statue unfreezing and presses his mouth to the Private's right ear. It is a long leaning, the man is so tall; he's like a birch tree bending into the wind. She can see his beard shuddering, giving off sound.

The Private's eyes roll toward the top of the cavern.

When the Nurse turns away from this strange confidence to mark the room of shades around her she sees they have closed in upon her position, ten feet closer than they'd been. There are more than just dozens of them, there are hundreds.

Maybe thousands—she's unsure.

She's going to seize the Private's hand and flee with him up the dirt shaft into moonlight when a slurry of pebbles and dirt hits the floor. The Quartermaster crashes in.

He looks a sodden, wretched fool, his uniform torn, his face covered in dirt.

The Nurse has never felt so glad to see another human being.

"What devil's trick is this?" he roars. "What motte-licking hog-swallow wimple-cock nonsense!"

He is blistering drunk and he flails through the dark, crashing and cursing among the stalagmites. The heads of the masked figures follow his progress.

He sees the Nurse and stops. "Not *you!*" he cries in agony.

He pinches the bridge of his nose with one hand and seems to crumple in defeat, kneeling ungainly in front of the Nurse, his clearly empty brandy flask, like a fallen knight's tribute, displayed in his palm. When he finally looks up and takes in the scene, the boot-flask clatters to the floor.

In the corner of the Nurse's eye: several figures muster out. These figures emerge from among the stalagmites bearing something enormous and square on their shoulders, one carrier each to the object's four corners. It is a sort of cage, she sees, which at first the Nurse judges to be made of bones. But then she sees it's made of muskets, bayonets still attached and sawed off at the stock. The faceless bearers set it down in the least crowded part of the floor and step back. Their manner is decorous—showman-like, almost.

Presenting: the cabinet that skins you alive.

Someone is meant to go in there. Someone is meant to not come out.

The Chaplain continues to speak to the Private, the beard-swallowed lips shuddering at the ear. Not terror but serenity begins to flood the Private's face.

The Nurse recognizes this look. She has seen it.

In the faces of men as they charge toward their deaths, as they lie in hospice, as the saw greets their limbs. It is unmitigated surrender to war, which is no less than war would have.

"Because you breathe and we do not," the Private translates haltingly, "we the dead do declare open war on the living." His mouth moves like a marionette's. "We consecrate this solemn act—"

But before he can get through the rest, they're upon him.

They fall on him and blot him out. It is as though they have lain dormant, withholding what now is a hideous strength, and they move with the long-muscled fierceness of jackals. Their teeth flash yellow in their masks. The Nurse can hear the Private grunting, trying not to scream. The jaws and the arms of the innermost horde are tearing at the Private's flesh while the rest moving outward are tearing each other, lashing out because they must. They're a grave-yard carnation that blooms in reverse; they come at him from every side. When the figures withdraw one by one from the Private, their mouths in their mask-holes are muzzled in blood.

The Chaplain is beside her now. His bearded mouth is at her ear. There is no more Private to tell her the rest so now she must hear from the Chaplain directly. His breath doesn't smell like stale air or decay; it's surprisingly sweet, like a loaf of bread, cooling.

The Nurse is keen to what he says, though he does not say words—not really. They occur to her that way because she is human, but when the words find her they do as sensation, the tortures of death and the shame of the damned, the purgatory of this place she stands in now beneath the hill, where these legions of Civil War dead have been waiting to make a claim upon a world they feel they owe nothing but what they have suffered, and listening to the Chaplain's sounds, the Nurse is subject to their meaning: the taking of the prisoner. The march upon the living world. *As above, so below,* flashes into her mind. How the taking of prisoners consecrates war and the terrible, sobering reason, she realizes at last, that she and the drunk man are both still alive.

"We must go," says the Nurse. "We must go right away."

But the words that come out of her mouth are all wrong; it is as though her speech were infected somehow with the dark and sensorial mush of the Chaplain, and it takes the Nurse all of a minute or more to even begin saying English again.

"Prisoner of war," the Nurse repeats, along with the phrase, "There can be no parlay," and how unless they "Fly, sir, fly!" then one of them must stay "in forfeit." The figures are circling them, licking their lips. Their rickety prison of muskets swings open. "I shall stay," she says somehow. "For I am meant to stay, you see."

The Quartermaster rises now. He says, "For once, I see your point."

But then he does the strangest thing: he pushes her out of the tightening throng.

She stumbles away and the figures part for her, revealing the shaft that leads back to the world—a world she suspects is beginning to brighten, the workers stirring in their tents "Go!" He shouts it. "Get you gone!" He flings his wrist across the room in a fey, disingenuous show of impatience. He flings it like he did before when he had told her, "Have your camp," and the Nurse had been certain a more hateful man existed nowhere on this earth.

At the edge of the cavern she stops and turns back.

If she climbs up the shaft it amounts to a crossing: one day she awoke in her bed and was good, the next day she no longer was. Yet the Nurse also knows if she doesn't go now she'll be cheating the world of the person she is and the person, always, she has known she will be, for she will have to warn them of it, she will have to lead the charge. Not just when the living come under the tooth and the Nurse must be called on to bandage their wounds but when they must beat the dead back from their borders—when the next generation embarks its campaign on the sons and the husbands, the brothers and friends, whose light they are learning to still live without. She does it for them and does it for this: the fragile Republic, just out of her reach.

The Quartermaster sees her stop, but then he makes it easy for her. He strides through the figures, who paw at his arms. He ducks his head into the cage; he sits cross-legged, petulant. He grits his teeth and slaps his knees. He roars, "Come and take it, you arshole-faced devils!"

The rank of figures nearest him begins to move upon the cage.

What happens next is very fast: she is clawing her way up the shaft to the surface. Screams echo up from the base of the dark. The lantern, still around her wrist, disintegrates against the rock and a shower of little glass pieces go by her, tinkling into the torchlight below. A few of them catch in her knees and she bleeds, and one of her fingernails snaps to the bed, and when she turns around again she is mounting the top of the shaft toward the daylight, a slug's trail of blood leading up the shaft's barrel where the strange, patch-work faces have yet to appear.

The Nurse moves forward, numbly twisting. Eyes vacant and

strange behind cascading dirt.

Someone on the surface will be there to greet her—someone from the company. They will steady her tumbling out of the hole. She will march down the hill with this man at her side to the place where the others have gathered their camp and here the Nurse will stand a moment, watching them watching her for the words she will say, but the Nurse will sense only how wretched she looks: her pale and daylight-flinching face, her skirts ripped in places and covered in dirt and flecked at the hem with the blood of the Private. None of this will faze the men, or seem to faze them, peering blankly— ready to go home or ready to dig, whichever one she tells them first. She will think of the Private the last time she saw him, a skeleton covered in streaks of red jelly, and also of the Quartermaster, his eyes peering out through the bars of his cage. But she will mention none of this. Instead she will call out, "Cold water. Who has it?" and the men will move backward, allowing her room. Any moment, she knows, she must say it, she must: what they both dread and long to hear. The armistice is over now. They are going back to war.

ACKNOWLEDGMENTS

This is always impossible, but here goes.

To all the editors who published these freakish, creature-forward stories over the last twenty years, but especially Halimah Marcus of *Electric Literature*, Jason Teal of *Heavy Feather Review*, Lincoln Michel and Nadxieli Nieto, and J.W. McCormack of *Conjunctions* and *The Baffler*.

To Brian Evenson, Yuri Herrera, Jac Jemc and Laura Van Den Berg for the gracious, generous blurbs. I revere all of you, each in your own way.

To my writing life correspondents: Bennett Sims (email), Laura Goode (phone), Ryan Bradford (both) and Patrick Michael Finn (Zoom). It's always a pleasure to read and hear your words.

To my oldest and most loyal friend, Aaron Pores, for reading pretty much everything I publish and always having something nice to say about it even when it's meh.

To Diane Goettel of Black Lawrence Press. Your support of my work means everything.

To the beta-readers of these stories, who helped me marshal their shaggy pelts into something suitable for a reader's eyes: Darcy Roake, Lincoln Michel, Jim Ruland, and Selena Anderson.

To my writing community and creative co-conspirators, the No-Name Writing Group of New Orleans, Louisiana for their thoughtfulness and exactitude, their candor, and their warmth: Tom Andes, Julia Carey, Anya Groner, Jessie Morgan, Rachel Nelson, Brad Richard, and Sheila Sundar. I consider you among my closest friends.

To my parents, Marjorie Milstein and Eric Van Young. I couldn't imagine this writer life without either of you and your bottomless love and encouragement. The same goes for my sister, Marin Van Young—and to my big-hearted extended family, all voracious read-ers themselves unfazed by my affable morbidity: Jo Anne Roake, Michael Roake, Jessica Roake, Dan Check and Stephen Stewart.

To my children, Sebastian and August Roake Van Young, for taking me out of myself every day while also providing me the space, energy and inspiration to travel inward.

To my partner, my best friend, my horror co-pilot, and my first reader, always: Darcy Roake. None of this could happen without you, nor would I want it to.

ADRIAN VAN YOUNG is the author of *The Man Who Noticed Everything*, *Shadows in Summerland*, and *Midnight Self*, as well as *Vampire Pool Party*, a book for children. His fiction, non-fiction & criticism have appeared in *Electric Literature's Recommended Reading*, *Guernica*, *BOMB*, *Granta*, *McSweeney's*, and *The New Yorker* online, among other venues. He teaches high school Creative Writing and English and lives in New Orleans with his family. More at: adrianvanyoung.com.